OPERATION
ARCTIC
DECEPTION

a Poppy McVie adventure

OPERATION
ARCTIC
DECEPTION

KIMBERLI A. BINDSCHATEL

Turning Leaf Books • Traverse City, MI

Published by Turning Leaf Productions, LLC.
Traverse City, Michigan

www.PoppyMcVie.com
www.KimberliBindschatel.com

Print ISBN-13:9780996189095
Print ISBN-10:0996189092

This is a work of fiction. Names, characters, businesses, places, events and incidents are either the products of the author's imagination or used in a fictitious manner. Any resemblance to actual persons, living or dead, or actual events is purely coincidental.

Thank you for purchasing this book and supporting an indie author.

For Rachel—
Thanks for sticking with me and Poppy.
She has that extra sparkle because of you.
For that, I'm forever grateful.

And to the brave men and women of the U.S.F.W.S. and their counterparts around the globe who dedicate their lives to save animals from harm. Their courage and commitment is nothing short of inspiring.

May their efforts not be in vain.

A woman is like a tea bag - you can't tell how strong
she is until you put her in hot water.

~Eleanor Roosevelt

OPERATION ARCTIC DECEPTION

CHAPTER 1

"You call this a date?" I said to Dalton as the door slammed behind us with a whoosh-bang.

The place was a back alley, hole-in-the-wall, with sticky floors and the unmistakable odor of fifty-some years of cigarette smoke mixed with fryer grease and stale beer. Every square inch of wall was covered with either a mirror emblazoned with a beer logo or a bumper sticker.

Dalton turned to look at me with those eyes. "Who said anything about a date?" He motioned toward a corner booth. "Let's sit there," he mumbled and moved toward it, casually assessing the other occupants of the bar.

"Seriously?" I muttered, and followed, doing the same thing.

Two men, in their thirties, built like construction workers, played pool on the far side of the room. An older man, not so fit, had both hands wrapped around a mug at the end of the bar, his eyes glued to a tiny TV that hung in the corner.

As Dalton approached the left seat of the booth, I grabbed his arm. "I want that side."

"Nope," he said with a grin, and eased into the booth where he'd been headed. "I'm not sitting with my back to the door."

My hands landed on my hips. "Well, neither am I."

"One of us has to." The grin grew more mischievous. "Since I'm already here, I guess you'll have to trust my keen sense of observation."

The door slammed shut again. I spun to see a grizzled man in his late sixties sauntering toward a barstool. The bartender had the top popped on a bottle of Miller Lite, and the bottle placed on the bar before he got there.

"Fine." I plopped down in the seat. "I've got other senses to rely on, not to mention my cat-like reflexes."

"Don't I know it." He gave me that look—the one that says we have something special between us, something intimate.

And we did. That was the problem. Dalton and I were federal agents and he was my partner. Recently, during an undercover operation together, we'd let our attraction for each other get away from us. And we almost got killed. I was still sorting out what to do about it.

"So, what are we doing here?" I asked.

The bartender, a young lady with thick eyeliner and hoop earrings the size of drink coasters, appeared at our table. "What can I get 'cha? We got Lakefront Brewery's River West Stein and Eazy Teazy Ale on tap."

"How are your burgers?" Dalton asked.

She shrugged. "Ah-right I guess."

"Do you have a vegetarian option?" I asked. It was worth a shot.

She scrunched up her nose. "Seriously? This is Milwaukee."

"A basket of fries and two waters," Dalton said.

She scribbled on her order pad.

"A couple Jello shots? The Badgers are playing."

"Right," I said, glancing at the TV. "No thanks."

Another shrug and she turned back toward the bar.

I crossed my arms. "So?"

"So, since we were in town—"

"In town? We report to our new team in Chicago tomorrow. We're two hours drive north."

"Anyway," he went on, ignoring me. "When I first started

at Fish & Wildlife, I worked for a time up north of here, near Manitowoc. It was a joint thing with Wisconsin DNR. My partner and I nailed a guy for poaching, but—" he winced with the memory "—the bastard got off on a technicality."

"That sucks." I didn't know what else to say. Dalton wasn't exactly the kind of guy who welcomed affectionate reassurance.

He stared at me for a long moment, drew in a long breath. "It was my fault."

I gave no reaction, tried to hide my surprise. Dalton was a former Navy SEAL who thrived on perfection, order, procedure. Admitting a mistake, well, I'd never witnessed that before.

"Yeah, well, my old partner has never given up. Apparently, the guy, Steve's his name, bought this place and has been using the walk-in here to store illegal meat. Sells it to restaurants with wild game on the menu. Anyway, a warrant's been issued."

"For today? Aren't you afraid he'll see you and bolt?"

"I was told to c'mon in."

The door made a whoosh-bang and I turned in my seat. A man in a Carhartt coat with salt and pepper hair, cut high and tight, strode toward us.

"Dalton, you old bastard," he said, grinning.

Dalton rose to shake his hand, but got pulled into a man hug with a lot of back patting.

The guy's eyes swung toward me. "And who is this lovely lady?"

"My partner," Dalton said. "Special Agent Poppy McVie. Poppy, this is Carl Thompson, Conservation Warden, Wisconsin DNR."

"Partner, eh?" His eyes lingered on me a little too long. "How come I've never been assigned a partner as good looking as you? I always get stuck with the likes-a Dalton here. Sum-bitches that you'd rather not see by the light of day." He chuckled, amused with himself.

"Indeed," I said, and summoned my best librarian voice. "Good thing for Dalton, the latest update to the Fish & Wildlife Employment Hiring and Compensation Code, Rule 247, Section three, under Eligibility and Exemptions requires a minimum sex appeal, as rated by the International Organization on Attractiveness."

Dalton managed to hold back a grin.

"Right." Carl didn't seem to get my joke. "Anyway," he went on, digging a folded document from his inside coat pocket. He handed it to Dalton. "We thought, since you was here, we'd let you serve him. For old times' sake."

"Well, damn, Carl. That's…" Dalton looked down at paper in his hands. "That's really thoughtful."

"He'll be here any minute." Carl held up his phone. "I've got a plainclothes out back. That's where he always pulls up. I'll get a text the moment he comes in the back door."

Dalton sat back down, and Carl invited himself to sit next to me. I slid over, allowing him room.

"Aren't you worried about someone alerting the perp?" I asked. "I mean, the staff here—"

"Naw," he said, shooing away any doubt with a flick of his wrist. "Everybody's in the loop. We've been working on this for years. We didn't mess around. The case is sewn up from every angle. We don't have to catch him red-handed." He leaned back, smirked. "This is for fun really."

His full attention turned to me. "So, I never would have guessed you're a Special Agent. You're so young, and, well"—his eyes dropped to my breasts, then quickly back to my eyes—"not exactly the type."

"Well, that's just it," I said. "They never suspect. It's a great advantage for undercover work."

"Poppy's being humble," Dalton said. "She's an excellent agent with superb instinct. Best partner I've ever had."

My mouth dropped open. Dalton and I had a rough beginning to our partnership, and I knew he'd come to accept me, even like me. But he'd never said words like those before.

Carl grinned at me. "Well, it seems our boy is as smitten with you as I am."

"Oh, it's strictly professional," I managed.

Carl threw his head back and roared. His laughter reached every dark corner of the room. "Well, I hope you can tame the boy. As I'm sure you already know, he can go off the rails sometimes."

I cocked my head to the side. "Off the rails? Dalton?"

His eyes landed on my red hair. "Though I bet you've got a bit of spunk yourself, eh?"

"You don't know the half of it," Dalton muttered.

The bartender plunked a glass on the table in front of Carl. Ginger ale, I assumed. And our fries and glasses of water. Without a word, he gave Carl a nod of respect and went back behind the bar.

"I'd never met a young man with such potential," Carl went on. "And, whew, the passion. He was gung-ho from the get go, like a horse just been let out of the barn. I had to rein him in on several oh-kay-sions." He leaned toward me like he was telling me a secret. "Patience was not his strong suit."

"Dalton?" I said, incredulous. He wasn't describing the Dalton I knew.

"He learned after Steve though." He glanced at Dalton, grinned. "He tell you the story?"

"He said he got off on a technicality."

"Hee, hee. Well, that much is true."

"We don't really need to go into it," Dalton said with a shake of his head.

Carl took one of the fries, crammed it into his mouth, and kept talking. "We was knee deep in mud. It was raining icy sleet like a sumbitch. Something like, I don't know, seven degrees. I'm about to lose my fingers from frostbite and Dalton looks snug as a bug in a rug."

He crammed a couple more fries into his mouth. "Did I

mention he's a crazy bastard?" he said, then snarfed down the fries. "So, we's out there, waiting for hours, 'cause we knew Steve'd be coming through with a boatload of illegal waterfowl. See, there was this narrow spot where he had to lift the motor and use an oar to push through the weeds, and we figured that'd be where we'd catch 'em."

He tipped back the ginger ale and drained the whole glass.

"Anyways,—" he set the glass down and held his fist to his chest, holding back a burp "—here comes Steve, just like we figured. But when he gets the nose of his rowboat into the weeds, he sees us. Or just gets skittish. Whatever, who knows. He's a squirrelly bastard. So, anyways, he throws that little outboard motor into reverse. Well, Dalton ain't having it. He plunges through the weeds after him. He's up to his eyeballs in water, but somehow manages to get a grip on the edge of that boat."

He shook his head and grinned with amusement. "Here's where it gets good. Steve doesn't know quite what to do. He's got a hundred-sixty pound weight on the side of his boat and water coming in. So, Steve, he—" Carl held his hand over his mouth and chuckled. "Steve's gotta get Dalton to let go, right? So, what does he do?" He chuckled again. "He stands up. Well, Dalton knows a little about physics, weights and balances and such, so he goes ahead and volunteers to let go, right then. Steve goes ass over tea kettle into the drink. Course he comes up cursing Dalton's ancestors, all in a fit of rage, and no doubt hyper-ventilating. Dumbass goes after Dalton. You see, Steve was nineteen and all of a hundred twenty pounds soaking wet. And Dalton was—" he gestured toward him "—I mean, the man's a Navy SEAL." He paused. "You know he was a SEAL, right?"

I nodded, but didn't want to speak for fear he'd stop talking. I was getting a glimpse of a side of Dalton I'd never seen.

Dalton pushed the fry basket toward Carl, saying, "Then we arrested him and took him in."

"Well, I couldn't see that good from my position, what with the freezing rain and such, you know, but I'm quite sure, officially—" he winked "—when Steve slipped, he knocked his head on the side of the boat. Then he ended up spending some time under water. Not too long. Just enough to change his perspective, know what I mean. Next thing I see, Dalton's flipped him into the boat. That Steve flopped around in there like a hooked fish.

"By the time we got him to the police station, his lips was blue and he was shivering like a Quaker."

He shook his head like that was the end of the story.

"So, what was the technicality?" I asked.

He shrugged. "We didn't have any evidence."

"He didn't have any illegal waterfowl after all?"

"Oh, he did. But when Dalton swamped the boat, they got washed out. Musta sank. He would'a had 'em tied with weights already, in case he came upon the law and had to ditch 'em quickly. You see, perps do that kinda thing all the time. They know the law. It's your job to dot your I's and cross your T's. Well, Dalton, he found out the hard way. The whiny little shit claimed unnecessary roughness, and since we didn't have no evidence, the judge was none too happy 'bout it." His phone chirped. He glanced at the screen. "Well, partner. You're on. He's in the kitchen."

Dalton took hold of the document and slid out of the booth.

Carl grinned after him, but made no effort to slide out of the seat. He leaned over to me and whispered, "That judge gave Dalton a real talking to. But now he's going to get the last—"

"Let me out!" I gave him a shove. "Where he goes, I go."

"You are something," I heard him say to my backside.

Dalton strode through the swing door, and I zipped in behind him.

Sure enough, a stocky, ape-of-a-man was headed for the walk-in.

Dalton brought him to a halt with his voice, stern and direct.

"Steve Scripnick, you're under arrest."

Steve spun around. His eyes found Dalton and a look of confusion came over him. He scrunched up his eyebrows, cocked his head to the side. "What the hell?"

"So, you remember me."

"Aw, shit." His eyes started to dart about. He was going to bolt. He swung toward the back door where the plainclothes officer now stood. Dalton moved toward him, but I stayed where I was, at the kitchen door.

Steve's eyes swung around to me, assessing.

"I wouldn't mess with her," Dalton warned.

Steve didn't seem like the brightest bulb, but I could see why he thought coming my way was his best option.

He barreled toward me like a bull out of the gate.

I planted my feet, dropped one shoulder and he hit me like a freshman linebacker. I shifted, trapped his elbow and pinned his foot, using his momentum to take him to the ground. He was a scrapper though. He rolled, knocking over a bucket of grease, and, surprisingly, sprang right back to his feet, though his hand caught the prep table. Two burger baskets flipped into the air. Fries flew every which way.

"Hey!" the cook yelled.

That must've given Steve an idea, because he picked up a mayonnaise-slathered burger and threw it at me. Smacked me right on the neck. I wiped the slime away with the back of my hand. He lunged and grabbed me by the hair with both hands.

Oh, no way, buddy!

My knee came up hard with a jolt to the groin. He let go. He seemed to fold forward with surrender, but he'd pissed me off. I grabbed the back of his head and dropped him on his face.

He lifted himself up on his hands and knees, heaving to catch his breath.

Then whack! The jerk collapsed into a roll, knocking me out at the knees and taking me down with him. I landed flat on my back in a puddle of grease, my hair all mashed into it.

"You shouldda seen that one coming, McVie," I heard Dalton say, with way too much amusement.

"This is getting downright entertaining." The plainclothes added. "We could open up the back door and charge admission."

I spun to my belly, got to my knees, grabbed hold of the bucket, and whacked Steve upside the head with it. The last of the grease splattered down his chest.

He bucked, tried to get up, but I was on my feet.

I planted my heel in his spine. "Don't even think about it."

Dalton grinned beside me. "I'm so turned on right now."

I wiped grease from my forehead. "Can't we go on a normal date some time?"

CHAPTER 2

Chicago. Rows and rows of tall buildings, sectioned into a grid. Throngs of people, hurrying to and fro. Noise day and night—cars honking, sirens blaring, trucks jacking their brakes. And the smells. Oh, the smells. Rotting garbage mixed with car exhaust and a hint of sewage. Big city.

What snow there was, had turned to icy, gray clumps that clung to the curb. Snowflakes didn't fall. They seemed to settle, uneasily.

I was out of my element.

Give me a blue sky and the rich tapestry of a deciduous forest. Or the open air of the sea. Or the varied greens of the jungle with the constant hum of insects and chatter of birds making their living in the everlasting cycle of life. The smell of fresh earth.

But the city was where the offenders were. This was where they built their networks of crime and destruction. Where wild animals, once trafficked or poached, ended up.

This was where we'd catch the bad guys. At least this time. These were the end users. The buyers. Those who created the demand.

Dalton and I had been assigned to an elite unit, a Presidential task force, created solely to investigate animal-related cases. It was a big honor, and I was determined not to screw up.

So, here we were. Unfortunately, our last two cases had

come down, one right after the other, in a whirlwind, and I felt like I'd been on a dead run. The lack of information heading into this was unnerving. But I'd had to wing it before. I could wing it again.

I was given a time to report to the downtown Chicago headquarters. Dalton's appointment was after mine. We weren't sure why we weren't scheduled to arrive together, but my latest goal was to follow orders, ask no questions.

The one thing I did know, and it was the best news of all, was that my new boss was a woman. Ms. Benetta Hyland. I couldn't wait to meet her. A woman! My hands felt clammy; I was so excited. This new assignment was everything I'd ever dreamed of, and I was determined to be a stellar employee. It would be so much easier with a woman at the helm.

Though I couldn't find any personal information about her, I did learn that she had been appointed to lead this task force after a twenty-year career in conservation. A leading national expert on the Endangered Species Act, she'd even testified before Congress. She'd also been a representative of the United States at the International Convention on International Trade in Endangered Species of Wild Fauna and Flora. She knew animal law, that was sure. And she fought for animals, just like me.

The downtown Chicago office was a huge, industrial-looking building among the plaza of federal offices across the street from Calder's Flamingo, the famous bright red sculpture.

I arrived on time to the office number I'd been given. It was a large room with eight cubicles set up in two rows of four. The sign on the door read, *Case Analysts*.

"Excuse me. I was told to report here, but I'm sure I must have the wrong office," I said, hoping someone would direct me.

A young man, younger than me, pushed back from his desk, rode his roller chair out of the cubicle, and looked up at me. He shoved his wire-rimmed glasses up the bridge of his nose.

"You the new intern?"

"What? No. Do I look like I'm—" I shook my head. "I'm from Special Ops."

His eyes narrowed. "Are you sure?"

I blinked once. *Am I sure?* "That's why I'm good at my job." I batted my eyelashes and flashed a fake grin. "No one suspects little old me."

"Well," he said, his head slowly easing into a nod. "You gotta talk to Greg for your assignment." His head swiveled on his neck. "Yo! Greg!"

A head popped up over a divider. "Yeah?"

"This girl is here for her report."

Girl? What was it with this guy? He was younger than me.

Greg's head disappeared like a prairie dog, back down its hole. The first guy didn't say anything more. He rolled back inside his cubicle, his eyes already glued back on his monitor, so I went ahead to Greg's cubicle.

"Nice digs," I said. A flat out lie. If I had to spend eight hours a day in this ten by ten, with its grey fabric walls and nothing but the glow of a computer screen, I'd be at risk of shoving an icepick in my eye. "I'm Special Agent Poppy McVie from Special Ops. I was told to—"

He sat up straight on the edge of his chair. "Special Ops, eh?" he said, entirely too impressed. This guy had to have been fresh out of school. His shirt was starched and pressed and buttoned tight at the neck.

"Are you the analyst for our mission?"

"Maybe. You got a case number?" he said, fondling his mouse.

"I wasn't given a number. I've been assigned to the Presidential Task Force."

His eyes lit with excitement. He leaned forward and whispered, "Oh *that* case. You're Poppy?"

I couldn't help myself. I leaned forward and whispered back, "Yes. I'm Special Agent Poppy McVie."

A silly grin spread across his pimpled face. He spun around in his chair and plunked away at his keyboard. Then he handed me a headset, typed some more, and spun back around. "It's ringing."

"Who are we calling?"

"Your new boss. That's what I was told to do."

"Okay."

After four rings, a female voice on the line said, "Hyland."

"Hello, this is Special Agent Poppy McVie."

"Yes. McVie. Sorry I couldn't be there to greet you in person. I'm stuck here in Washington. I'm glad to have you on the team, though. You've come highly recommended."

"Thank you, ma'am."

"Sorry, I know this is a little unorthodox, but, there it is. With your experience, I'm confident you can jump right in."

"Yes, ma'am."

"We're tying up loose ends on current operations, still pulling the team together. I'd like you to help out with a current operation. Greg will bring you up to speed with your assignment details. Go ahead and get settled in, and we'll meet when I'm in town next week."

"Yes, ma'am. Am I to—?"

The line was dead.

Greg leaned my way, eyebrows raised.

I yanked the headset off my head. Damn thing got all tangled in my hair.

Greg was staring at me, expectant.

I tried to hide my disappointment. "She said to get the details from you."

"Right on," he said and spun around on his chair. His fingers rattled the keyboard.

I grabbed a hold of a bunch of hair with my left hand and tried to work the headset out with the other. Finally, I slammed it down on his desk, now in pieces, a knot of hair still stuck in it.

Greg ignored the headset and spun back around to face me.

"A few of the members of your new team have been working on a sting here in Chicago for a few months now." He explained that a taxidermist had been busted for mounting illegal species, and they'd been building a case on every poacher who'd come through his shop. Dalton and I were being worked into the scheme. The hope was that we'd be able to help flesh out the last of the targets before the big takedown, which was planned to happen in another two to eight weeks.

"You're going to work at Wilson's Taxidermy Shop."

I stared at him. "A taxidermy shop? Are you sure? I have no knowledge about taxidermy whatsoever." *And I find it disgustingly macabre.*

"That's okay. You only need to actually work as the counter girl."

Girl, again? I refrained from informing him how annoyingly offensive that was. "What's my directive?"

"Hyland thought that a new person working in the shop, with fresh eyes, might see something that has been missed."

"Anything else?"

"And you're to play the new girlfriend of Special Agent Michael Wessell."

"And my directive for that?"

He read from the monitor. "Says here, keep a lookout for anything that might have been missed."

"Right." Translation: they didn't know what else to do with me.

"And lastly, you're to keep a close eye on the proprietor of the shop, Jim Wilson. He's on electronic tether, but it's always good to have human intel as well. You're to—"

"Use my fresh eyes to see anything that might have been missed?"

He nodded.

"Right."

Wilson's Taxidermy shop was right in downtown Chicago, south of the river, tucked in between an old shoe store and a tobacconist. All three were red brick with signs made and hung around 1940.

With all the cash flowing through the place, I'd pictured a modern building with shiny floors and glass cases.

The odor was the most unexpected part. All the carcasses and hides made the whole shop smell of damp animal. It was an earthy smell. Not exactly unpleasant. More like an old, wet goat had been living in a root cellar that never got aired out.

"You get used to it," Jim said as he gave me the grand tour of his shop.

"I don't know," I said. "It's so…"

"It's like anything else. Your brain starts to tune it out." He stood, cross-armed. "So we should probably get right to teaching you the customer service stuff, eh?"

"Actually, I'd really like to hear your story first. If you don't mind."

A frown creased his brow and his eyes turned soft with sadness. "All right. C'mon. We best stay in the back room for that one. We can keep an eye on the front door from there."

I followed him to the back, past the workroom where hides hung on drying racks next to the salt table, past the bench where they'd be stretched onto the molds and all the detail work done.

He poured and offered me a cup of coffee, which I accepted, then poured a second. He set up a folding chair, gestured for me to sit, then pulled up a stool and eased onto it. His cat, a brown and black Maine coon, leapt onto his lap and Jim's hand automatically started stroking its ears.

Jim was in his late sixties. A short, hefty guy with a white beard. Put him in a red velvet suit and he'd easily pass for old Saint Nick. He even had rosy cheeks and a hearty chuckle.

"I've owned this business for forty-two years." His eyes traveled around the room as though every good memory was being conjured right then and there. "Me and the wife, we started it from nothing. I'd been a taxi driver before that, but due to some health issues, I had to give it up. Taxidermy was just a hobby, but I started doing some work for friends, on a count of having time on my hands, you know. Then one thing led to another and before you know it, we had us a full blown business."

He smiled then. "I suppose it was a dream I'd never admitted I'd had, making a living outta doing something I loved. The years went by. We didn't make much money, but somehow we were able to make ends meet." A shrug of resignation. "Then it happened."

He took a long draw of the hot coffee as I waited, wondering what his version of the story would be. Jim had been busted for illegal wildlife trafficking and his shop seized. It was now under ownership of the federal government and Jim was a probationer. At least that was my impression. The report from Greg the analyst had been light on particulars.

Obviously, Jim had struck some kind of deal, because here he was, drinking a cup of coffee in his shop rather than sitting in a prison cell. I wasn't sure how I felt about that yet. But there was something about Jim. I liked him the moment I'd met him. And not just because he reminded me of Santa.

"Then what happened?" I urged.

"My bride. She got the cancer. Doctors said they could help, with some pills. Expensive pills. But we didn't have no insurance. Not enough anyway."

He took another swig of coffee and hung his head, running his hand down the cat's back. Avoiding my eyes, he said, "We was desperate, you know." Then he lifted his gaze, looked me right in the eye. "And I'd do it again, I guess."

The bell that hung over the front door jingled. He and I looked to the monitor. A customer had entered the shop. One man, alone.

"Oh, it's him again," Jim muttered.

"Who?"

Jim shook his head. "I think his name is Hal. Odd guy."

"You're not sure of his name? I thought you had documentation of all your customers, so they could be investigated."

He shrugged. "He's never bought nothing. Just comes in, hangs around, generally wastes my time."

I watched on the monitor as the man moseyed in, casually looking around.

"Well, let's get to it," Jim said. He gently placed the cat on the floor then rose from the stool and headed for the front room, coffee cup in hand.

I followed.

"Mornin' to ya," Jim said as he passed through the doorway. "How can I help ya?"

"Just stopping in," the man said, his eyes roaming over the many mounted animal heads that hung on the walls. Then he seemed to search through the full-body displays on the floor— a lioness, two black bears and a six-by-six elk. "Got any new ones? Anything exotic?"

"I been busy, but nothing I can think of since you were in last."

"Uh huh," he breathed and scratched his head. "Any good stories?"

"Not really." Jim obviously had no interest in engaging with the guy.

Hal, if that was his name, seemed like the stereotypical used-car salesman. Smarmy. He was dressed in polyester slacks and a thin, white button-down shirt, though he didn't wear a tie. I got the feeling he was headed to work and would put it on at the last minute. He was not an executive or highly educated engineer-type. Definitely a salesman of some kind.

"Are you a hunter?" I asked.

He came to a halt as his eyes settled on me, as if he hadn't realized I was in the room. "No, not really. Well, yeah. Birds." He nodded as though convincing himself. "I'm not very good at it." He licked his lips. "Not like these guys." He made a vague gesture toward some of the bigger mounts. "That's something, to go to Africa and take down a lion like that. To kill that kinda beast. Man, that'd be something."

I controlled my urge to explain how *it'd be something* to take him down with a roundhouse kick to the head, let him see how that felt.

"I'd love to meet the guy did that," he continued, with nauseating awe.

"Can't help you there," Jim said. "If that's all, I got work to do."

Hal shrugged, seemingly oblivious to Jim's annoyance. "So, you the new girl?"

What's with everyone calling me a girl? "Yeah," I managed. "My first day."

He nodded, but said nothing more.

"If you're interested in meeting other hunters," I said, "why don't you try the Safari Club?"

"The what?"

"The Safari Club. It's an international group of hunters. They have annual conventions, fundraiser banquets and such." We had a team member working that angle as part of the sting. "I mean, if you want to meet other hunters around here. I'm sure, if you look online, you could find a local chapter."

"Ah." He nodded, thinking, then seemed to drift off. He poked around the shop for another two minutes, then moseyed back out the door.

"So you're saying he never brings anything in?" I said to Jim.

He huffed. "Takes all kinds, I guess."

We returned to the chair and stool in the back, refilled our cups with coffee and resumed our conversation.

"Anyway, where was I?" Jim asked, sitting back down on the stool. The cat appeared and was back on his lap in an instant.

"Your wife was diagnosed with cancer."

"Yeah, well, long story short, guy comes in with a couple of untagged deer. I explain how it's illegal and he could get in trouble. That was always my policy. Then he offers me cash to do the work anyway. A handful of it. Well, those pills Alice was needing cost a helluva lot of money." His eyes got glossy and he blinked several times. "I figured, one time, just one time, and that'd be it."

I nodded in understanding.

"Next thing I know, I'm hiding all kinds of illegal species, running 'em in and out the back door. I got guys coming to me from three states away." He sighed. "Still it wasn't enough. I lost my Alice anyway. The drugs just made way for some faster, more aggressive kind of cancer. Like that, she was gone."

"I'm so sorry, sir."

He snugged the cat close to his chest. "Masie here is all I got left of my Alice. She was her darling."

His eyes got misty and I felt like I was intruding on his memories.

"Well, anyway," he said, coming around, "two days after her funeral, Special Agent Mike Wessell shows up in my shop. I guess he'd been watching me for some time, gathering evidence. I felt like such a fool."

"Then you went to court and the judge—"

"No. I never went to court. Never had no lawyer neither. I was never arrested."

I sat back in the chair. That didn't make any sense.

"Wessell turned my open sign to closed, showed me his badge, and said I had to go with him. With Alice gone, I didn't really care what happened, so I didn't question nothing. That's when I met Benetta Hyland. I believe she's your new boss."

I nodded.

"She explained my situation, how she could send me to prison for years, but she had some sympathy for me, I guess. She offered me a deal. I keep running the shop, like nothing happened, don't tell nobody nothing, and your unit has full control, all the records, everything. I get to keep doing the work and no prison. Well, how could I say no?"

He set the cup down and glanced at a portrait on the wall. Alice, I assumed.

"I never wanted to do wrong to begin with. I just wanted to save my Alice. I suppose I got a chance now to make it right." He pushed his foot out from the stool, pulled up his pant leg. The cat sprang from his lap. "They make me wear this here ankle bracelet." He huffed. "Where'em I gonna go anyway?"

The bell at the door chimed again.

"This is what I do," he said and pushed himself up off the stool and headed for the front room.

CHAPTER 3

I climbed the stairs to the secret room that had been built in the attic by the government, once they took ownership. The walls were covered with monitors that received a live feed from the cameras hidden all over the shop. I could keep an eye on Jim from here, though it was obvious he was fully compliant.

My job for the next few days was to become educated on the main targets of the sting operation—in case any came into the shop. Then I could—do what exactly?

I sat down at the computer, pulled up the files, and scrolled through some images.

It seems Wilson's Taxidermy, without Jim even realizing, had become a stop on a main highway for illegal wildlife trafficking. Maybe not a stop, but certainly the narrow part of a funnel, the perfect crossroad for us to analyze the action.

Like Jim had said, Ms. Hyland could have put him behind bars for a long time. He'd broken the law. But, in many ways, he was a little fish. And my new boss wanted to catch a whale. Jim's web of connections was the net she would use to do it.

Some of the members of my new team had been integrated into that web. Top of the list for me to get to know was Special Agent Michael Wessell. His cover was a wealthy stock trader who liked big hunts. He attended several different Safari Club chapter meetings, held poker parties, hung out at the gun range, and the like. His objective: get to know the players, befriend them. And I was to be his new girlfriend.

There wasn't much in his file. No photo. And I could find nothing on the Internet, which was expected. All undercover agents' personal info, including mine, was redacted from the internet by the agency for our protection.

I wondered what he was like and was reminded of my very first operation when I had been assigned to play Dalton's wife. We'd never met, and I'd assumed he was some middle-aged, overweight, gray-haired hard ass, but it turned out he was a sexy-as-hell, buffed out, ex-Navy-SEAL hard ass that I couldn't seem to keep my hands off. I've been sorting out what to do about that ever since.

And now, I was to play the girlfriend of another agent, one I didn't know, all the while hiding being the real girlfriend of my partner.

Wait. Was that what I was? Dalton's girlfriend? I guess we hadn't exactly put words to it. He and I simply had... a thing. A secret thing. So secret, I wasn't sure what it was.

The bell on the door jingled, and I checked the monitor. It was Dalton, carrying a paper bag.

The other customer had come and gone. Dalton was alone in the showroom. "I got it," I hollered to Jim and headed to greet Dalton.

He was admiring the mounts. "The guy does nice work."

"He's a nice man, too," I said, keeping my voice low. "The babysitting part of my job is going to be easy."

"Yeah, what about the staying out of trouble part?" he said with a straight face.

"Very funny." Somehow my hands landed on my hips. "So did you get your assignment?"

"Yep. I'm a hunting guide. Big connections. Easily bribed. Whatever you want to shoot as long as my palm is greased. Heavily. Hey, kinda like you last night."

"Again. Very funny." I'd resorted to using Dawn dish soap to get the lard out of my hair.

He grinned. "I thought we could study the players together." He held up the paper bag. "I brought sandwiches."

"Sure, yeah." The thought of hanging out in that tiny surveillance room with Dalton made my nerves tingle.

"So, are you going to show me around, or what?"

"Sure, yeah. This is the showroom, the retail area, I guess you'd say. Jim calls it the front room. Most of these mounts are from last year. The hunters have been notified to come by and pick them up. I can't believe what he gets for this. Thousands of dollars. And that's for the legal ones."

"Men like their trophies."

"Don't I know it."

"Anyway, I still have to learn the paperwork, how to take in a carcass, how it needs to be tagged. The usual stuff as if I really worked here. I might need to know it if Jim gets sick or something. And it's part of my cover. I'm just glad I'm not expected to help with the actual mounting work. We've got a contractor for that." I led him to the workroom. "That's the salting table. Jim peels the hide off the carcass—" my lip curled up in revulsion "—as far back as needed for the kind of mount they want. That's called the cape, I think."

"That's right," Jim said, coming around the corner from the bathroom. He held out his hand. "I'm Jim Wilson, glad to meet you."

"Special Agent Dalton, Poppy's partner."

"I bet you miss her already. She sure is a breath of fresh air."

I couldn't help but grin.

"She is that," Dalton said with a genuine smile. "Nice to meet you, Chief."

Jim cocked his head to the side.

"Your tattoo," Dalton said.

Jim looked down at his own forearm and the anchor tattoo—an insignia of a Chief Petty Officer. "Huh. I haven't been called Chief in a long time."

"Where'd you serve?" Dalton asked.

"My last tour was on the Forrestal. On the flight deck."
Dalton hesitated.

"Yeah, I was there, if that's what you're wondering."

"For what? What happened?" I asked.

Dalton shot me a look of warning.

"It's all right," Jim said. "It was a long time ago."

"There was a fire," Dalton said, his tone solemn. "A big one. On the flight deck."

"I lost some good friends that day."

"I'm sorry," I said, feeling ignorant and insensitive.

"How about you?" Jim asked Dalton. "You served, obviously."

"Frogman."

Jim's eyes grew wide. "Impressive."

"What's that?" Dalton asked, pointing at Jim's airbrush set up.

"Oh, that's what I use to paint the noses and around the eyes."

"You do nice work."

"Thank you, son. I try. Been at it many years. Always felt like it was an art, making them look as real and alive as possible. I want to capture the true beauty of the animal, you know."

I was taken aback by the irony. But that's what many hunters will say. That they admire the animal, its majesty. The well-known quote from the spiritual teacher, Osho, came to mind, about loving a flower. *If you pick it, it dies and ceases to be what you love. So let it be. Love is not possession. Love is appreciation.* That's what my dad had taught me. He'd gone after countless animals for a "trophy" photograph. It was all about appreciation. This concept of killing something, then preserving it in some fake pose, was so foreign to me, so *wrong*, so misplaced. I couldn't wrap my mind around it.

"It's the little things," he went on. He picked up a plastic mold of a nose. "I always cut out the septum. It doesn't look right. The deer's nose just isn't like that."

He had Dalton's interest.

"And the ears. I've got my own way'a settin' them, too."

"I can see why you've had a thriving business here," Dalton said in admiration.

"Yeah, well." Jim shrugged, his gaze dropping to the floor.

"You've been a great help with the operation so far, I'm told," I said, trying to give him some redemption.

That brought his eyes up and a nod. "I'm doing what I can."

"Well, uh, we're going to study the case together. In the surveillance room." I crossed my arms. "Just letting you know. That's where we'll be. Working." Why did I feel like I was talking to my dad?

Jim grinned. "You kids run along. I've got work of my own, too."

I grabbed the stool and led Dalton to the surveillance room.

"There's not much room up here," I said. "But we should be able to manage."

With all the monitors running, and being in the attic, the room was stuffy and at least eighty degrees. "Did you bring drinks, too?"

"Iced tea."

I grinned. My favorite.

He plopped the bag on the desk. "So, you figure out yet who's the head honcho around here? Who's breaking the most laws? The one you're going to start pestering me about?"

His ever-so-slight grin clued me in that he was teasing. "I have. Coincidently, he drives a rowboat, so you're going to come in handy when the time comes to nab him."

His grin disappeared.

I cocked my head to the side. "What?"

Deadpan. "Not funny."

"It's hilarious. Knowing you were once a little overzealous, too." I gave him a smile. "Now I know you're human."

He took a sandwich from the bag and dropped it on the desk in front of me. "Eat."

"Well, if you're gonna be touchy about it." I tore the wrapping from my sandwich. "If you must know, my plan is to watch and observe."

"Isn't that redundant?"

"It might be, but that's my directive, and I plan to do my job."

He stared at me, waiting. Then said, "Are you saying you'll follow the rules? You're not already itching for some action? You're going to do exactly as you're told?"

I looked him in the eye. "I'm not going to screw this up."

I took the chair and nibbled at my lunch while Dalton gobbled his as he balanced on the stool.

His mouth stuffed with a ham and Swiss on rye, he asked, "What's with all the monitors?"

"Part of my job is to keep a close eye on Jim, but every camera is also recording. I swear, they have nearly every corner covered."

He nodded, shoved the last of the sandwich into his mouth.

Jim was on the move, headed for the staircase. "Hey, Poppy!" he shouted.

"Yeah," I replied, heading halfway down. He'd already told me he wasn't going to try to make the climb.

"I need to run down to the post office. And I'm going to stop at the butcher shop. If someone comes in, tell 'em I ran for lunch, and I'll be right back."

I'd already been made aware of his regular routines, which were allowed to continue uninterrupted, and this was expected. "All right," I said. "Thanks for letting me know."

We watched him go out the front door.

"Well, where do you want to start?" I said to Dalton.

His eyes settled on me. Those eyes. With that look.

"What?" My insides flushed with warmth.

He lifted one eyebrow.

"I told you, right? That every room in this place, including this one, is under video surveillance."

"Every one?"

"Yes," I said, nodding. "Well, except the landing on the staircase. It's a black hole."

"Where? Show me?"

Was he up to what I thought he was up to?

I got up and went half way down the stairs. "Here. See, no camera has a view."

He pressed against my back, pushed my hair out of the way with his nose and nuzzled my neck. "So, no one can see us right now?" he whispered.

His hands gripped my hips and he spun me around so fast it made me dizzy. "As long as we stand right here? Is that right? Make sure to squeeze in, close together?"

His lips were an inch from mine, his eyes deep into my eyes.

"Yeah," I managed. "Right. Here."

"Good to know," he said, his breath warm on my face.

"In case, we…"

"Mm, hmm." And he kissed me. *God, this man can kiss!* Even my toes felt it. My head got light as surges of passion pulsed through me.

I wrapped my hands around his neck. I wanted more. I pulled him closer and he pulled me closer, pressed me tight against his hard body.

His fingers gently dug at my hair as he held my head, kissing me harder.

I was on fire!

Jingle, jingle. The front door swung open.

I pulled away from Dalton, breathless. *Dammit!*

Footsteps, toward the back room. "Forgot my damn mail. Swear I'm losing my mind."

Jim. Back already.

I flew up the stairs, Dalton headed down.

"Hey, uh, where's the head?" I heard Dalton say.

Jim must've pointed. I didn't hear a response. Back at the monitors, I saw him pick up some envelopes from the table and head back out.

I drew in a deep breath. *McVie, get it together.*

When Dalton got back, he sat down on the stool, all professional again. "Shall we get to work?"

"Good idea."

I'd been alone with Dalton in the car, on the drive all the way to Milwaukee, then back, then he'd dropped me at my hotel room. We could have spent the night together. But we didn't. Neither one of us had said anything, nor made a move. Not a peep. I'd started to wonder if I'd imagined everything between us. Or if he'd changed his mind about me.

Then *that* just happened? I closed my eyes. *God, I'm no good at this.*

Boyfriends weren't exactly my forte. In fact, I'd never really had one. Not a serious, honest-to-goodness boyfriend. The kind who meets your mom, goes to Christmas dinner, buys you Valentine's Day presents. I'd always been too... driven? Chris, my best friend, says I scare them away. That I'm a strong, independent woman with a mind of her own and most men can't handle that. Maybe that's true. Feels more like it's because I'm awkward.

My long red hair expands to double size with the slightest hint of humidity. You can find well-known constellations among my freckles. I've even been known to confuse a handshake with a punch and taken a guy to the mat. That doesn't usually go over well. *No guy wants to feel inferior.* My mom's voice.

My dad always told me to be true to my heart. To be me. And if I wanted a man in my life, the right one would come along. Was that Dalton? I swear, most times he's more aggravating than not. He pushes my buttons. All of them.

I sat up straight. *How does he do that? I'm usually so... in control.*

Dammit!

"Okay, so." I put on my professional face. "Apparently, the sting revolves around the shop here. A lot of the players are connected. One of our new teammates, Special Agent Mike Wessell, is set up as some wealthy big wig, making pals. Going by the name, get this, Mike Stetson."

Dalton grinned.

"He's the one who busted Jim."

"Really? Hm."

"Why? Do you know him?"

"No. Our paths crossed at the office. But I didn't realize who he was." He gave no hint of an opinion one way or the other.

I took a long drink of iced tea. Man, it was hot in here. "Well, I'm supposed to be his girlfriend."

Dalton tensed, ever so slightly. He turned and looked at me. "Poor sucker has no idea what he's in for."

"Very funny." I gulped down some tea.

"The plan seems to be that once all the players are identified and evidence catalogued, a massive list of warrants will be issued and simultaneously served. That way no one can alert anyone else. It will be a complete surprise. That is going to be one exciting day, don't you think?"

Dalton nodded, interested.

"But still, I get the sense from the directives here, that arresting all those criminals isn't the end goal. There's information about some mysterious kingpin who's figured out a way to bypass customs and illegally import. That's the guy Ms. Hyland is after. Seems all the rest of this is to get information to seek and destroy that one man."

"She sounds a little like you," Dalton said.

"How do you mean?"

"Well, driven. Singularly focused. Big picture thinker."

I nodded. Those were good traits.

"Delusional," he added.

I frowned. "Thanks."

I shifted in the chair, then grabbed the mouse and clicked through some folders, bringing up still photos that had been extracted from the videos taken with the hidden cameras in the taxidermy shop. "This guy is a known poacher. Frank Lutz. Apparently he's got a big mouth. Our man Wessell has been partying with him, getting the scoop on others. These three"—I pointed at another photo—"are Larry, Eric, and Mark. They're Frank wannabes. Typical behavior. Treat women like objects and animals even worse."

"Nice crowd."

"They all have notes in the files. Drugs, underage girls. You name it. But they've never been caught. Not your typical lowlife dirtbags. These are lower forms of dirtbag. They're more devious. And more rich."

Dalton nodded.

"Frank is a dentist. Owns eight locations. He's dropped over $150,000 on three hunts that we know of. All illegal species. Larry's a radiologist, Eric day trades, and Mark is spending daddy's money. Mike has logged suspicions about all three, stories the team hasn't been able to corroborate. But apparently, they're suspect enough to be targeted for the sting."

"Sounds good," Dalton said.

I pointed to a folder labeled *Law Abiding*. "There are hundreds of video clips of customers. They all have IDs that correspond with Jim's client file, where he's got all their contact info. We can cross match any of these photos by the assigned ID with catalogued video."

He pointed to a folder labeled with a question mark. "What's in there?"

I clicked on it. The files had no IDs. "I'm not sure."

"If they don't have IDs, does that mean the customers are unidentifiable?"

"I guess so."

Dalton sat back, crossed his arms. "Why would someone go to a taxidermy shop if they didn't have taxidermy work? It's not exactly a place you just browse around."

I clicked on the first video and it started to play. The front door opened. A man came in, looked around. "Hey, that's Hal," I said. "I recognize that mosey."

"Who's Hal?"

"I don't know. He came in this morning. Jim doesn't know him either. He says he just hangs around, asks random questions. Never has any work for him. Generally annoying."

Dalton shrugged. "Some people are odd."

"He seemed in awe of the big game hunters, but, I don't know. It didn't seem—"

"Oh, no. Here we go," Dalton groaned.

"Hey. Isn't it my job to be suspicious? Look at everything with fresh eyes?"

"Yeah, but—"

"But nothing. That's my directive. And that's what I'm going to do." I clicked on another clip. It was Hal again.

There were twenty-seven clips of him. Each time he came in to the shop, milled around, asked random questions, like Jim had said, then left without any transaction.

"What do you want?" I said to the image on the monitor.

"Dunno." Dalton answered. "But he's said nothing incriminating. He doesn't even give any sign that he's interested in taxidermy."

"Then what?"

"Like I said, some people are just odd. Doesn't make him a criminal." He pointed at another folder on the desktop. "Let's get back to studying the players the team has identified."

"Right," I said, nodding. But something about Hal niggled at me.

CHAPTER 4

After several hours, I thought my eyeballs might dry up and fall out of my face. "Let's take a break," I said, and went down the stairs to stretch.

Jim had a hot glue gun in one hand and a paintbrush in the other, working on a turkey.

I came to a halt, turned to him. "I thought you said you didn't do birds."

"I don't, usually. But this is for a long time customer. He insisted I do it for him. Not my best work, though."

"You usually refer customers with birds to another shop, though, right?"

He set down the glue gun. "It's all been documented. Your team's been watching his shop, too."

"Oh I know." I paused, thinking. "That Hal guy, who came in earlier. When I asked him, he said he hunts birds. He ever ask you about doing one?"

Jim thought a moment. "Dunno."

"Does he know you don't do them?"

He shook his head. "Dunno."

I didn't remember him asking in any of the videos. I'd have to look again. But maybe that explained it. Maybe he kept coming back to see if Jim mounted birds. Maybe?

According to the reports, Jim usually locked up and went home at six. Someone, somewhere at headquarters—Greg probably—tracked his whereabouts until the next morning, so I was off the hook until then.

At five thirty, Dirk arrived. Since Jim had grown the business with both legal and illegal species, the workload had become too much for him to handle alone. Headquarters didn't want to turn anyone away and miss an opportunity, so they hired Dirk to work second shift to keep up. In fact, I was told, it had been the bane of the project. Too much actual, legal work to manage.

Dirk wasn't an agent, but a trusted contractor. I believe his sworn agreement went something like, "I ain't talking to nobody about nothing." And when he walked in the door, I believed it. He had a way about him.

He must have been at least fifty, had a loping gait, eyeglasses designed circa 1970, and, from the look of his skin and the raspy cough, a three-pack-a-day smoking habit. He worked ten-hour shifts, Monday through Thursday, and played jazz at some downtown club on the weekends.

Jim introduced him to Dalton and me.

"Hey," said Dirk.

"Hey," Dalton replied.

Men.

Dalton turned to me. "I'll catch you later. At the meeting."

Tonight Dalton and I were to meet Mike, my pretend boyfriend, and Tom, another team member. Tom's role had been a mobile taxidermy delivery service driver, a set up nicely positioned for him to investigate other taxidermists in the area—easy access to the backrooms, where he could see all.

"Uh, sure? Wait. I thought you'd drive."

I was also supposed to move in with Mike, since I was playing his girlfriend. Apparently he had some house as part of his cover and I needed to get out of the hotel anyway.

"I've got an errand to run. You can take the train right?"

"I guess." Why couldn't I go on the errand with him?

Jim grabbed his coat. "I'm beat," he said. "I'll walk out with you." They headed for the back door. "See you tomorrow," Jim said over his shoulder.

As the door closed behind him, I heard the jingle of the front door. "I'll get it," I told Dirk.

With a smile, ready to greet the next customer, I pushed through the door to find Hal. He was standing next to the full elk mount, reading the tag, odd as ever.

"You're back again," I said. "You must work close by?"

"Nah, well, yeah. On my dinner break."

"Well, how can I help you?"

He shrugged. "What was that club you told me about this morning? I forgot."

"The Safari Club?" He'd come back just to ask me that again? Or was that an excuse?

"Yeah, that was it." He looked around the room, for what I couldn't tell. "Thanks." He moved toward the door.

"All right then," I said. "Glad to help." What was he up to?

Something wasn't right about this guy.

He pushed the door open and was gone.

I rushed to the back room. "Dirk, I need you to close up. I've got to run." I grabbed my coat and purse.

"But I'm not supposed to—"

"Just close early then," I shouted over my shoulder as I ran out the front door.

He'd gone right. I thought.

Darn it! The cat had followed me out. I scooped Masie up in my arms and she yowled and squirmed. I shoved her back inside, pulled the door shut, and spun around.

The rush hour crowd bustled to and fro on the sidewalk. What had he been wearing? A black coat. That didn't help.

It was already dark and the rush hour traffic grumbled through the streets. Why were they constantly honking?

There he was, half a block ahead. I closed the distance in double time. He was hoofing it along. For a guy who seemed to live in mosey-mode, he sure was quick on the street.

My cell phone rang. I grabbed it. "Yell-o."

"Special Agent McVie?"

"Yeah." I didn't recognize the voice.

"This is Special Agent Brown."

Brown? Brown? Um?

At the next corner, Hal turned left and crossed the street with the light. I had to hurry to make it behind him. He never looked back, which was good. There wasn't a tree anywhere to duck behind.

"Tom Brown. I do the mobile taxidermy service."

"Oh, right!"

Hal stopped. I stopped. What was he doing?

"Where are you?"

"Just out for a walk."

Hal got moving again.

"I see. Well, you're headed over to Mike's place for the meeting, right? I thought I could pick you up, save you the train ride."

Hal made a right turn, crossing the street. I had to jaywalk to keep up with him. A horn blared at me. "Hey buddy, I had plenty of time!"

"Maybe you shouldn't be walking and talking?"

"It's fine. I'm just in a hurry."

"I thought I'd catch you at the shop, but it sounds like you're busy."

"Yeah, I was there. But now—I'm running an errand."

"Sure. Sure. I'll just see you there." And he ended the call.

I stared down at the phone in my hand for a moment. *Crap.* Not the best first impression.

One more block and Hal turned into a building. An old, indistinct brick building, three stories high. I waited until the door closed behind him before moving close enough to read the tiny sign bolted to the door. It read, "Elite Children's Parties." Children's parties? This guy was some sort of party planner? For the rich?

I stared at the sign. What'd that have to do with anything? Maybe he *was* just an odd duck, like Dalton said.

After getting off the northbound train out of the city, I hailed a taxi and hurried into the backseat, snowflakes swirling in with me. I gave the driver the address of Wessell's place. Soon we were headed north again, into the sprawling suburbs.

The houses got bigger and bigger until finally we turned into a drive and rolled to a stop in front of a giant wrought-iron gate. The driver spun in his seat. "This it?"

I wasn't sure.

A man in a uniform pushed open a door-sized gate that hung to the left of the main gate. He walked up to the car, opened the back door, and said, "Good evening, Miss Poppy."

"Good evening to you," I chirped, as though we were old friends.

"Thanks for the lift," I said to the driver as I dug around in my purse for some cash. The guard got my suitcase and shut the door behind me.

"Right this way."

I followed him through the gate to where a golf cart awaited, all enclosed with thick, clear plastic to protect from the winter weather. He gestured toward it. "Your chariot, m'lady." I curtseyed before taking my seat, he got in the other side, pressed on the pedal, it whirred to life, and we puttered along to the main house.

Something was amiss. Before me, a contemporary-style mansion, at least 25,000 square feet, sat perched on a hill overlooking Lake Michigan. The grounds were several acres with, I'd guess, at least five hundred feet of frontage. I couldn't see a house to the north or south. This was quite the high-priced chunk of property. There was no way the bureau was paying for this place. Even for a Presidential task force.

The guard brought the cart to a halt at the door and got out, came around to my side, and peeled back the plastic door for me. "M'lady," he said as he gestured for me to disembark.

The door to the house swung open. "Welcome! C'mon in. Come in out of that cold." I assumed this was Mike. He was about Dalton's age, but not quite his build. Thinner, more of an urbanite. Dark hair and eyes. Italian descent. Not unattractive.

He waved enthusiastically, as if the motion would hurry my way.

I didn't want to say anything yet, ask any questions, as I didn't know what the guard knew. I bid him goodbye with a thanks and hurried inside.

Then I stopped short, eyes wide. On one side of the foyer stood a full mounted lion, his bushy mane brushed out to accentuate the king of the jungle's crowning glory. His head was astounding. I'd seen many pictures and videos, but I had no idea the sheer size of a male lion's skull. And its jaws and teeth.

On the other side of the foyer was an ostrich. The thing stood eight feet tall. It was posed as though mid-stride. Who hunts an ostrich? Seriously?

"Yeah, I know," the man said, as though reading my mind, and held out his hand. "I'm Mike."

I shook it. "Poppy."

"This is all part of the dog and pony show. Wait 'till you see the secret trophy room. That one will really get you."

I nodded, though not sure I wanted to.

He took a step back, looked me up and down. "So you're the legendary Poppy McVie."

I gulped in air. *What?*

"Oh, I know all about how you caught Goldman."

"You do?"

"Yeah, that Dalton. Good guy. Humble. Said it was all you."

"He did?"

He'd talked to Dalton? "Well, Dalton, yeah, you're right. He is too humble. Doesn't take the deserved credit."

Mike raised one eyebrow. A grin formed at the corner of his mouth. "Ah, so you two, uh, you're—"

"Oh, no." I shook my head. Too much? "Nothing like that. We just, he's a great agent. I've learned a lot from him. It was just circumstance, is all. I was the one who ended up in the right place at the right time. But without his support—"

Mike wore an expression of amusement.

Damn. I'd said too much. I had to let it go.

"Can I get you anything? You thirsty? Hot cocoa?"

"Maybe some tea?" Why had Dalton lied to me? He *had* talked to Mike and didn't tell me.

He went to an intercom on the wall, pressed the button, and spoke. "Annette, would you please put on some tea? Thank you."

"You have a housekeeper?" I asked, incredulous. This was way too elaborate of a set up for a government operation.

"I know. I'll never get an undercover gig like this again." He gave me a warm, conspiratorial smile. "And you get to play my girlfriend. What do you think about that?"

"I'm not sure yet," I said with honesty.

"It was my idea. I figured you'd be bored to death, stuck down there at the shop, babysitting Jim. Was I right?"

I nodded. That was true.

"This way, you can get a peek at the players. Witness the action."

"I appreciate that." *Witness? Not get in on?*

He gestured for me to follow him into the living room which was larger than a bus station. Big, plush couches, positioned to form a square in the center, anchored the room. They faced the windows for the best view of the lake. One corner had a built-in bar, the other a TV the size of a ball-park Megatron.

Between the two corners, along the back wall, an array of woodland animals was staged to rival any Cabela's store display in the country. Three white-tail deer grazed. A black bear clung to a tree trunk above a raccoon, a fox, and two wolves. I was torn by the beauty of the presentation and the disturbing purpose, the animals frozen in eternity, ripped from life to be forever a trophy display.

"I hope you'll be able to hide that expression when it counts," he said.

"What?" I spun to face him.

"You're obviously disgusted." He said it with a tone of concern as he made his way to the bar.

"No, I mean, yes. What is all this? How'd you end up with this house? This mansion? These mounts?"

He grabbed a bottle of beer from the refrigerator, popped the top, took a sip, and said, "That's a great story. This place is owned by a famous movie star. I'm not supposed to reveal who, but, believe me, you know him. Anyway, John, an old partner of mine, he knew a guy who knew a guy. That guy, he told the owner that we needed a place to make my cover believable, could he help. Not only has he given us use of this place for the duration of the sting, he's continued to pay his security and staff—"

A young woman approached with a tray holding one cup of tea.

"Speaking of, this is Annette." He gestured toward me. "This is Poppy, my girlfriend." He put emphasis on the word girlfriend, making it clear that the staff was in on the nature of the situation.

I thanked her for the tea and she disappeared once again.

"We've done background checks and they've been sworn in. We debated whether we should keep up the cover for them as well, but decided that since they know who really owns the place, not me, they already knew something was up. They have directive to keep eyes and ears open whenever we have visitors."

"Gotcha," I said, still amazed at the set up. "So you're actually living here for this operation?"

A grin spread across his face. "I know. It's too good to be true. I missed out on the summer fun though. You should see the boathouse."

"I bet."

"Anyway, all the mounts were brought in from the repository. I admit, I've been having fun making up the stories for each of them. That lion in the foyer, whew, was that an exciting safari hunt. The man-eater nearly devoured my hunting buddy. Knocked him over, but kept coming for me. I got off three rounds before he dropped at my feet."

He paused. I must have been scowling. "What? It's called method acting."

"I understand. I'm sorry. I didn't mean to be—" I looked over at the wolf, its head mounted low, like it was stalking, its mouth fixed in a permanent snarl. "I just find all this repulsive."

"Yeah, well, me too. That's why we're going to catch the bastards, eh?"

I nodded. Smiled.

"I've heard a lot about you," he said with a hint of admiration, as if it were all good.

"I've heard a lot about you, too." It was somewhat true. I'd heard he busted Jim. And Jim had told me he'd had no idea that Mike was an agent. "Completely bamboozled," had been his exact words.

"You certainly have been an asset to Fish and Wildlife. I'm honored to work with you."

I grinned and my cheeks started to flush. I didn't know what to say.

"So I was thinking maybe we should spend some time to get to know each other, since we are to be dating for this op and all. Sound good?"

"Sure," I said, nodding.

"Later, I mean. After the meeting."

"Right, yes," I said. After the meeting. I was to meet some of the other team members tonight at their regular debriefing.

They'd give updates and bring Dalton and me up to speed.

"I ordered pizzas," he said and took another swig of his beer.

Something about his attitude felt freeing. This was all fun for him. He obviously took the job very seriously, or he wouldn't be in the position he was in. But it was a game. An acting job. Swindling the swindlers. So different than Dalton's serious, hard-core SEAL approach.

I felt myself relax a little. "You got another one of those?" I asked, nodding toward his beer.

His lips widened into a big grin. "One for the lady."

A buzzer buzzed as he popped the top.

"Tom's here," he said. "You'll like him. Good guy. Sharp as they come."

We moved toward the door. Tom let himself in, brushing snow from his coat as he entered with one hand, holding pizzas in the other. The door hung open behind him.

"Hey, hey, hey," Mike said. "This isn't a barn."

Tom spun around and slammed the door. "Whew, it's nippy out there tonight." He turned back around and honed right in on me. "You must be Poppy."

I followed the two of them to the living room where Tom set down the pizzas, wiped his hands on his pants, then offered his hand.

He had a firm handshake.

"So how long have you been an agent?" I asked him. He wasn't much older than Mike.

He'd worked his entire career for Fish & Wildlife, while Mike had come from drug enforcement. He went on, something about training then different posts.

Had Dalton talked to Tom, too? Why hadn't he told me about it?

"Right, Poppy?"

"Huh?"

Tom's eyebrows shot up. "My career path isn't that confusing."

"Right. No. I'm just feeling a little weird that you two seem to know me, but I don't know you at all."

He gave me a big grin. "That's why we're here." He turned to Mike. "I need a beer."

Without hesitation, he got his own from the refrigerator behind the bar. "Have you shown her the secret room yet?" he asked.

Mike shook his head. "She just got here. Bring your beer and let's go."

Tom popped the top on a bottle and led the way up a grand set of stairs, down a hall, to a room on the back side of the house. "We set this up so Mike could really sink the hook in 'em."

He pushed the door open and I followed him in.

My mouth dropped open. I was speechless.

"Yep, I knew it would getcha," Mike muttered.

At the center of the room stood a full African-bush elephant, its long husks sharpened to a deadly point. To one side, a polar bear stood on its hind legs, its mouth contorted into a roar. On the other side, a cheetah frozen in mid-stride. It looked small and awkward in comparison. I guess it's hard to portray a sixty-mile-an-hour sprint, its true glory, in a mount.

All furniture that might have adorned this room had been removed. Along the walls were glass display cases. It was like a museum of dead animals, all lined up for viewing like pottery or sculptures.

On the wall hung a black rhino head, its horn intact, and beside that, a bald eagle.

"Tell me the men who really killed these animals are in jail."

Tom shrugged. "Who knows. These all came from the Colorado repository. Confiscated somehow or other."

"You should spend some time in here," Mike suggested. "Work on your poker face."

"I'll be fine," I snapped. I turned to see his expression. "I mean, it just makes me angry. Sorry."

He brushed it off. "Yeah, I'm getting tired of saying, 'If it flies, it dies.'"

"A bald eagle," I said, shaking my head. "Why?"

"Actually," Tom said, "I caught a guy once with a bald eagle. Helluva story. Back when I was a field officer. I hear shots when I'm out patrolling, so I go investigate. It happened to be turkey season, but I watch this guy walk up to an eagle he'd shot and put in a burlap bag. I made myself known, told him to open the bag. Well, he gives me some crap about needing a warrant. I, of course, calmly explain that I have probable cause. You know how they love that. I saw it, I says. So open the bag." He made a lopsided grin. "Anyway, the son-of-a-bitch pulls his side arm on me, says 'There ain't nothing in the bag' as he waves his pistol in the air, like he's some kind of Jedi knight and just saying so makes it true. Says I better back away or he'll blow my nuts off. One twitch and I could kiss my balls goodbye." His hands instinctively moved to protect that area now. "A man with a gun pointed at your balls can be quite convincing. I admit, I retreated, hands at my crotch."

He smirked. "As soon as I could, I called in backup. The guy was so cocky, instead of ditching the bird, he'd sauntered to his vehicle, thinking he'd scared me off. We made the arrest and he threatened me. He'd didn't mince words, neither. In front of the other agent. He got five months jail time, but I still get threats from him to this day. Nasty too. He threatens my wife." He grinned. "The man should do his homework. I've never been married. But still."

"Geez," I said. "How'd he find you?"

Tom shrugged. "He got my name on the arrest report. It's a hazard of the job." He took a sip of his beer. "I miss those days in the field."

"I know what you mean," I said.

Dalton walked into the room.

"Hey, man," Tom said.

Dalton nodded. "Housekeeper let me in."

"You get a beer?"

He held up a bottle.

"Well, I suppose we should actually have a meeting."

I stood there another moment, staring at the elephant, wondering how they got that huge animal in here, anyway.

Dalton whispered in my ear, "The legs are removable."

I spun to face him.

"Yes—" a wink "—I can read your mind."

"Am I really that obvious?" Maybe I did need to work on my poker face.

He shook his head. "I just know you."

We made our way back to the living room and sprawled out on the couches.

Tom started. "I got nothing new to report. Truly, I'm making my pay burning gas, driving around Chicago on icy streets." He glowered at Mike as he grabbed two pieces of pizza and folded them over to cram in his mouth. "I still don't know how you got this house gig and I got stuck in the van."

Mike shrugged. "It's all about charisma, man."

"Charisma, my ass," he said with a mouth full of pizza.

Mike ignored him. "I'm planning a guys' night. Been working some new suspects and having Dalton on board, as the hunting guide, is the ticket, I think. There's a wild game banquet next weekend. I'll make the last of the invites there. Then we'll seal it up." He eyed Dalton. "Why don't we bring you to the banquet, introduce the idea early. Maybe it'll get them intrigued, you know, to have a face on it."

Dalton nodded.

"Poppy and I are going to spend some time working on her cover as my girlfriend. We should be all set. Poppy's moving in here with me. Save on the budget."

Did I see Dalton flinch?

"Anything else? Questions?" Mike asked.

Dalton and I shook our heads.

"I'll leave you to it," Tom said and rose from the couch. He adjusted his jeans at his hips. "See you at the boss's meeting."

Dalton lingered, then said, "Poppy and I have been studying the suspects, getting up to speed. We'll be ready."

"Great," Mike said, rising from the couch—a hint for Dalton to go.

"So, I'll see ya," Dalton said. "You two be good."

I grinned. He didn't like me playing Mike's girlfriend. He didn't like it one bit.

CHAPTER 5

One thing was sure, working the counter in a taxidermy shop, coupled with hours of computer time studying the detailed comings and goings of poachers, gets to be rather dull. My mind kept wandering to figuring out what was going on between Dalton and me. Were we a couple or not? Sure, we had to keep it hidden, but keep what hidden? I wasn't even sure what to call it.

"We're going out to dinner," I told him on the phone. "It's a big city. No one will see us. And what if they do?"

It was a Thursday night and I'd found a local Italian place that touted handmade pasta and a legendary wine list.

"Pick me up at the shop at closing time."

"Yes, dear," he said.

"Are you mocking me?"

"Nope. Trying to be amicable."

Amicable? "Uh, okay." *Enough of this.* "This is a date. A real date."

"Uh, okay."

I clicked end. *That man!*

At five thirty, my phone rang. I grabbed it, and assuming it was Dalton, I said, "Don't tell me you're cancelling!"

"Huh? What?"

"Oh, sorry. Chris?"

"Yeah, what's up?"

Chris was my best friend. He'd just been through a difficult time—his fiancé, Doug, had died under terrifying circumstances—and I'd been worried about him. "I'm so glad you called. How are you?"

"Well, you're not going to believe it. I'm in Chicago."

"No way!" Chris was a flight attendant with Delta Airlines.

"I only have a few-hour layover. I'd love to see you. Can you meet me near the airport?"

"Of course!" He gave me directions to a little restaurant. "Oh, but—I had plans with Dalton."

"Plans? Like a date?" Chris said with a conspiratorial tone.

"Yeah, but you're more important."

"Bring him along."

I could. Yeah, that would work. He'd understand. He knew what Chris had been going through.

We pulled into the parking lot, right on time. Chris had chosen a little sandwich shop nestled among the row of hotels outside the airport.

I pushed through the door, Dalton right on my heels, and came to a halt. Dalton nearly ran right into me.

Sitting next to Chris was my mother. As usual, she was wearing her class A uniform, dripping with medals. I swear she slept in it.

My heart rate shot up. My teeth clenched. *Chris, I'm going to kill you.*

Chris wore the smile of a cat.

They both rose to greet us.

"Mom," I said. "What a surprise." I shot eye darts at Chris.

"Oh, don't be mad at Chris, dear," she said as she hugged me, rubbing my back like she always does. "You really should call your mother more often so she doesn't have to resort to these kinds of tactics." She turned to Dalton. "You must be Poppy's partner, Special Agent Dalton is it?"

"Yes, ma'am," Dalton said, respect in his voice. "It's an honor, Admiral McVie."

"At ease, sailor," she said, offering her hand.

"I'm pleased to meet you."

We all took our seats around the table, Dalton sitting as erect as a spine patient.

"So, Chris tells me you're a military man, a SEAL."

He nodded.

Of course my mother would set her sights on Dalton. She respected SEALs, as fighting men, but she'd made it very clear over the years that they were not eligible boyfriends for me. Too much testosterone and a natural inclination to seek trouble. Bad combination, she claimed. Chris better not have mentioned a word about our relationship or I'd kill him.

"And you're partnered with my Poppy," she said with a sympathetic smile. "I bet that's frustrating."

The burn started up my cheeks. "Mom. I'm sitting right here."

"Oh, don't get all uptight, dear. You know what I mean. He knows what I mean. He's a SEAL and you, well, you just march to the beat of your own drum, that's all." She interlaced her fingers in that annoying way. "Not exactly regimented."

"Yeah, well, regimented isn't all it's cracked up to be."

Dalton clammed up, crossed his hands in his lap.

Well, this was going great already.

"I'll order the sandwiches," Chris said, rising from his chair.

"I'll help you carry them," Dalton said, on his feet faster than Chris.

I waited for them to get out of earshot. "Mom, can you be any more rude?"

"What? I didn't say there was anything *wrong* with you. You're just different." She patted the back of my hand. "You're unique."

Eye roll.

"You got lucky to land such a capable partner. You've moved up fast. You're on this new team. I'm very proud of you."

I got the implication. "My advancement has nothing to do with Dalton. I've earned it on my own. Believe it or not, I'm actually very good at what I do."

"Well, I didn't mean it like that." She adjusted herself on her seat. "I just worry about you is all. This job is dangerous. Last week I heard about an agent who got shot in the head." She leaned toward me, changed her tone. "You know there are lots of ways you can save animals. You could become a lobbyist. You'd be a great lobbyist."

"You can't be serious." Of course she was serious.

"Or an executive director of one of the wildlife agencies. With your smarts, there's no doubt in my mind. And that passion. You'd have everyone all stirred up into a frenzy of action, signing petitions, sending letters to their congressmen—"

"Mom! How many times are we going to have this conversation?"

She pursed her lips. "You forget what happened to your father."

My face turned red. "I have not." My father had been killed by a poacher. But he wasn't a trained agent. He was a photographer.

"I just don't want that to happen to you."

Dalton and Chris returned with drinks in hand and set them on the table.

Chris gave me a tentative look.

"She thinks I should become a lobbyist," I said. "Write petitions."

He spun around. "Getting the sandwiches."

Dalton hesitated, his eyes following Chris, then must have decided that would be too obvious. He eased into his chair without making eye contact.

"Don't you agree, Dalton." My mother wasn't going to let up. "Certainly the field is not a place for a twenty-four year old girl."

Dalton had the look of a scared rabbit.

"We've been over this," I said. "I am not a *girl*. I'm a grown woman."

"Actually, ma'am," Dalton managed. "I'm quite comfortable with Poppy. She's proved to be more than capable. In fact, I can't think of anyone I'd rather have at my back."

My mother reared back, narrowed her eyes. "Are you sleeping with my daughter?"

Dalton's mouth dropped open.

"Mom!"

She waved it off. "Eh, I just wanted to see his face."

"That's not even funny."

Chris plopped the sandwiches on the table and dropped into his chair. "Actually, that was pretty funny."

I raised a finger to him. "You're in the doghouse."

"Oh, leave him be. He worries about you, just like I do. And I'm your mother. It's my prerogative."

I frowned. "You could have some faith in me, Mom." I turned to Dalton. "Like Dalton said, he trusts me."

Dalton had suddenly found that rearranging the pickles on his sub sandwich was very important.

"I'm a good agent. I'm making a difference. It's what I want. Why can't you just support me?"

She crossed her arms. "So, Dalton. I trust you'll keep an eye on her for me."

Dalton looked at me, managed a yes ma'am, then went back to examining his sandwich some more.

There was a long, awkward pause. My mother finally took a bite of her sandwich.

Dalton must have decided to make an attempt at a normal conversation, because he looked up and said, "You're at Walter Reed? Is that right? Head of orthopedic surgery?"

She turned to me, eyebrows raised. "So my daughter does acknowledge that I exist."

I forced a grin. I hadn't said a word about my mother to Dalton. He'd read my personnel file, which had ticked me off at the time.

I attacked my sandwich, trying to divert my anger.

"Well, this has been very nice," my mother said, looking at her watch. "But I must be getting back." She rose from her seat. Half of her sandwich lay uneaten on the table.

Dalton was on his feet. Military habit.

"You think about what I said," she told me, gave me a kiss on the cheek, and she was gone.

All the air left my lungs in one big whoosh.

Then my eyes narrowed and fixed on my best friend. "Chris, what the hell?"

"She practically begged me."

"You owe me. You owe me big."

Dalton grinned at me. "Well, that was fun."

CHAPTER 6

Turns out, Chris had more than a few-hour layover. He was actually off for three days. Dalton knew how much I'd been worried about Chris, so he scooted out, leaving us to talk.

"So you had a date planned, huh? Sorry about that," Chris said once Dalton was out the door.

"I guess. I'm not so sure he was all that thrilled about it."

"Are you two not…?"

I shrugged. "It's Dalton. You know how it is."

"I wish you two would just do the dirty and get it over with. You're driving me crazy."

"You are seriously on my shit list right now."

"Yeah, well."

"How have you been doing? Really?"

His eyes turned moist. "Surviving."

"One day at a time," I said.

"How's this gig? You knee deep in intrigue yet? Ready to pounce on the bad guys?"

"I wish. It's rather boring, to be honest. And you know I hate the city."

"Well, you're stepping into a long-term sting thing, right? All the players are already identified?"

"Yeah, mostly. Except there's this guy. Comes into the shop a lot. Doesn't buy. Just looks around, asks strange questions."

"Like what?"

"I don't know. About the hunters. Like he's some kind of trophy hunter groupie. It's weird. There's something off about him. He was in the other day and when he left, I followed him."

"Was that wise?"

"No. I don't know. But he's up to something."

Chris was shaking his head at me.

"What? I know something's fishy."

"Aren't you supposed to have probable cause or something like that?"

"I didn't search him. I just followed him down the sidewalk. And I found out he works at a hoity-toity children's party planning place."

"Party planning place? Say that ten times in a row."

"I'm serious. It doesn't make sense."

Chris shrugged. "What ever does?"

"I need to find out more." An idea sprang to my head and a grin spread across my face. "I think you've got a party to plan."

"What? No way."

"You owe me. Mom. Really? With Dalton there, too? What the hell?"

He frowned. "Fine. What do I have to do?"

"God, it smells like a Hungarian street fair in here," Chris said, his nose scrunched up.

"Yeah. I know. Now sit still."

"It's like a funeral home without the smell of carnations."

"Well, it kinda is."

"Do I really have to wear the wire? I mean, what if he sees it?"

"I want to hear everything. You might need coaching or something. We don't know what you'll see or hear."

"Coaching? No. Nope. No, no, no. No, there is no way. I'm not wearing an earpiece. Nope. That's where I draw the line."

"But Chris, I need—"

"Nope. My way or I'm not doing it."

I stared at him. "Why not?" I tucked the microphone under his collar. "Don't adjust your shirt."

"Because he might see it. Then what? I'm not getting hazardous duty pay here."

"He won't see it. Look at this thing." I held it up. "It's the size of a pin. I need to put it in your ear with tweezers."

"Are you serious?"

"Pretty cool, huh?"

"Is it clean? What if I get some ear fungus or something?"

I gave him a look. "Ear fungus?"

"Anything else?" he said, annoyed.

I held his head steady with one hand as I placed the device in his ear.

"Ok, let's test it." I put on the headphones with the built-in microphone. "Can you hear me now?"

"Just what I need," Chris said, nodding. "You right inside my head."

"Okay, your appointment is in twenty minutes. It's about a five-block walk. With the booster in your pocket, I should be able to monitor from here. So, remember what I said. Engage. Get him talking. Act like you've got all day to shoot the breeze. Maybe mention hunting. But don't be too obvious. See if you can't get him to talk about it. You know, maybe he'll give us a hint. Maybe if you—"

"Poppy, I got it."

"But don't be too obvious."

"I got it." He rose to go.

"Okay. Good luck."

"Here goes nothing," he said and headed down the stairs and out the door.

"Don't forget that if he starts—"

"Swear to God, I'll rip this thing from my ear."

"Gotcha."

In no time, he was at the building. The sounds of the street disappeared and I heard the click of a door.

"Say something," I told him.

"Like what?"

"Good. I can hear you loud and clear."

Another door shut. Then I waited. Chris hummed with the waiting room Muzak.

"Cut that out."

He hummed louder.

Finally, I heard Hal's voice, inviting him into his office.

Show time!

"So what brings you in today? Are you planning a birthday or other event?" Hal asked. He seemed much more articulate than the guy who'd lingered in the taxidermy shop.

"Yes," Chris replied. "A birthday. My nephew. Spoiled brat, actually. You know, parents who are never home. They throw money at him to make up for all the missing hours. It's got to be lavish. Excruciatingly so. Sky's the limit."

"Chris, don't overdo it," I said.

"Nothing's too good for their little monster."

"Ah," Hal said. "Believe me, I know what you mean. Lucky for you, that's exactly the kind of thing we handle everyday. Let me get our brochure. What age is your nephew?"

"Ummm." Chris hesitated.

"Ten," I said. I have no idea why. The number popped into my head.

"The big one-oh."

"That's such a fun age," Hal gushed.

The sounds of a chair being moved screeched in my headphones.

"Will it be boys and girls both? Adults, too? Or just for the kiddies? And what's the total head count of each?"

"Well, adults, I think, yes, then playtime for the kids, then cocktails for the adults," Chris said. "Definitely cocktails. Do you handle that, too?"

"I got you covered," Hal said, as if they were old friends. "Our company doesn't handle that directly, but we regularly subcontract this great caterer. I can set it all up as part of the package. No problem."

"Oh, great."

"What's your budget?"

"Oh, ten thousand?" He must have leaned forward or something because there was a crackling in the line. "Give or take a few thousand, of course."

My throat clenched. Good thing we weren't planning to actually book this thing.

"Ah," Hal said. "Well, I'm confident we'll come up with something really special for the birthday boy. Does he have any favorite characters? Disney or other? We have several themes to choose from."

Silence.

I couldn't come up with anything. What do kids that age like these days?

Finally, Chris said. "I don't know. I guess I need to find out." Then a pause. "He likes animals."

"Easy. Don't be too obvious," I whispered.

"Wildlife, actually. The kid stares out the window at the bird feeder like it's a video game."

Dammit!

"Got anything like that?"

"Not really," Hal said. "How about Harry Potter? All the kids like Harry Potter."

"Yeah, yeah," Chris said. "I forgot that. He's super into Harry Potter."

Hal went on to explain all the decorations and games that would be part of the package. I couldn't believe how elaborate these kids' parties could be. He went on and on. Gourmet cookies. Soda pop fountains.

"I need to run this by my sister, of course," Chris said, finally.

"Sure, sure," Hal replied.

"But you can go ahead and start writing it up."

Chairs scooted across a wood floor.

"I'll give you a call tomorrow," Chris said. "To firm everything up."

"Sounds great."

And he was on the street and headed back to the shop.

I was at the front door when he got there.

"What happened? You didn't mention hunting."

He shook his head. "Didn't feel right."

"Well, were there any hints in his office? Pictures of him hunting? Anything like that? I mean you could've—"

"No." He shrugged. "I don't know. We talked about kids' birthday parties. That was the point. I didn't know how to ask. I'm not exactly the type to be normally interested in hunting, you have to admit. It's not exactly a typical hobby among us gay guys."

I nodded. He was right.

He followed me up the stairs, back to the surveillance room, where I took out the earpiece.

"Sorry, Poppy. I don't know what to say. He was actually… nice. Quite charming to tell you the truth. Maybe there's nothing there."

I plopped down on the stool. "I was sure of it."

"Listen, you've got a good thing going here. You're on this elite team. Your career is on overdrive. Relax. You don't have anything to prove."

I crossed my arms over my chest. "Maybe you're right."

"Maybe you're looking too hard, starting to see things that aren't there."

But I knew something wasn't right. Hal was up to something. He had to be. My gut said so.

"Fine," I said. "Let's get some food. I found this great little Italian restaurant I've been wanting to try."

"That's a great idea," he said and was up and headed for the door.

We walked the ten blocks, our ears frozen and lips blue, but made it before all the tables were taken.

The wine list was twelve pages long. Twelve pages!

"You look as giddy as a dog with a new bone," Chris said.

"So, I love wine. So what?"

"Pick something before they update the list and we have to start over."

"You're forgetting. You're still in the doghouse."

"What? I thought that little trip to talk to the oddball party planner was a get-out-of-the-doghouse-free card."

"How'd she get to you, anyway?"

"She's worried. And so am I. I know you don't want to admit it, but what went down in Alaska in that grizzly camp was hardcore stuff, man. Then Mexico. I think you're in denial about it all."

"It's my job. I'm trained for it."

"Nobody trains to deal with the emotions for stuff like that."

"I'm fine."

"Are you?"

"Well, okay. Let's say for one moment that I'm not. My mom sure as hell isn't going to help matters."

Chris frowned. "Fair enough."

"So, why did you fall for it?"

"I think you should give your mom a chance. She's not that bad."

"Can we just order?"

Chris gave me a reluctant nod and busied himself with the menu.

When the waiter arrived, we were ready to order.

As soon as he walked away, Chris's phone rang.

"I think it's Hal," he said, surprised.

"Well, put it on speaker phone."

Chris hit the button. "Hello."

"Yeah, this is Hal, your party planner."

"Oh, hello Hal. What's up?"

"It's seems noisy there. Should I call back at another time?"

"No, nope." Chris grabbed the phone, clicked off speaker, and held it to his ear.

"That better?"

I held up my hands. What was he saying?

"Uh huh. Yep. Yeah." Chris nodded. "Yeah, they would. Yep."

I couldn't stand it.

Chris's eyes grew large, his mouth slowly opened. He stared at me.

"Do you mean a real one? Alive?" he said.

What? A live what?

"Yes, yes. I'm sure they'd be thrilled."

Thrilled about what?

"What are we talking, here? How much?"

I chewed on my thumbnail.

"I will let you know right away," Chris said and hung up.

"What? What'd he say?"

"Holy crap!" Chris said.

"Holy crap what? What? Tell me."

"He said he had a special offer for me, what with my nephew liking Harry Potter so much. Poppy, he offered to sell me a pet Hedwig. A live one."

I inched forward. "A what?"

"For five grand. A live Hedwig."

"What's a head wig?"

"Are you serious? A snowy owl. He's selling live owls as pets."

CHAPTER 7

I sat back in my chair. Stunned. I knew something was up, but—"Wow!"

"That's illegal, right?"

"Uh, yeah. Native owls are federally protected under the Migratory Bird Treaty Act. You can't even possess one of their feathers without a permit. Chris, this is big. Really big. I mean, he must have a source. How's he getting them? Transporting them? Snowy owls live in the arctic. There must be a whole network set up. He's not just selling one owl here."

He'd said he was a bird hunter. Was that a ruse? Was he snooping to see if Jim would mount birds? But he was selling them live. Why does he go to the shop then? What does one have to do with the other?

"Well, what do we do?" Chris asked.

"I don't know. I sure didn't expect this. I mean, holy crap. Snowy owls." I shifted forward in my seat, my brain switching into strategy mode. "Okay, you need to stall. Make him think you're really interested but at the same time be aloof. Can you do that?"

"I don't know. I guess so."

"I need to figure out why he is coming to the taxidermy shop."

Chris shrugged. "Can't help you there."

"Does he want to have some mounted? Maybe one that died

in transport? Does he think he'd still make some money selling stuffed owls?"

Chris shook his head.

The waiter appeared with the wine I'd ordered, a Frank Family Pinot Noir. He opened the bottle and poured each of us a glass.

I raised mine to Chris. "I ordered this wine to splurge. I didn't know I'd be making a toast for this."

Chris raised his glass and clinked mine. "No kidding."

The wine was earthy, with a hint of cinnamon and vanilla.

I held the glass in my hands, cherishing it. "Okay, I need to come up with a plan here."

"Do you? I mean, shouldn't you tell your new team about it? Then you all make a plan?"

"Well. Yeah, I guess so. You're right." I grinned. "They are going to flip out."

Our handmade pasta arrived. I gobbled it up, but didn't taste a thing; I was so excited. My first meeting with my new boss was tomorrow morning. I couldn't wait to tell her.

Today I was going to meet our new supervisor, the head of the team. My nerves turned my stomach sour.

I wanted to ask Mike about her, maybe get some insight, but he was gone already. He was a busy guy, I guess.

I made myself eat some granola and called it good.

Dalton picked me up, said he wanted to ride in together. The first thing he said to me when I opened the door was, "How's it going with Mike?"

"Okay, I guess." Was he jealous?

"What does that mean?"

"He's barely home. He wasn't here last night before I went to bed. Who knows where he was. Not my place to ask, I guess. He wasn't around this morning either."

Dalton seemed bothered by this. "So, you still haven't

worked on your cover stories yet?"

I shook my head. "He said we had plenty of time, not to worry, but, I don't know."

"Well, where's he been?"

"How should I know?"

"You didn't hear him come in last night? Or leave this morning?"

"Are you kidding? My room is five miles from the back door."

He looked around the immense foyer. "Good point."

I bid Annette goodbye and climbed into Dalton's car.

"Hey, how come you get a car and I don't?"

"Maybe they've seen you drive."

"Very funny."

When we arrived at the office, Tom and Mike were already there.

Dalton and I filled cracked, dingy mugs with coffee and found chairs around the table. They were government quality—hard-backed, no cushion at all. The fluorescent lighting gave all of us an unnatural pallor. It felt a lot like the interrogation rooms they show in the movies.

Tom and Mike hardly spoke. We waited. Stared into our cups.

Finally, the door opened and in strode my new boss, Benetta Hyland. She held herself erect, a formidable woman. In her mid-fifties. Maybe. Her attire wasn't terribly fashionable. Simply professional. Short hair. Conservative glasses. Nothing notable. The word sturdy came to mind. Like a horse. Though that wasn't to say she was unattractive.

She got right to it. No time for chitchat. All business. She headed toward the chair at the head of the table. Tom and Mike sat up straight. Dalton and I rose to greet her. She shook our hands, cordially. Not a warm welcome. Not a cold one. She reminded me of my mother, actually. All business.

"Dalton and McVie, welcome to the team. The president wanted you, so here you are." She nodded, as if that were an offer of acceptance. Then a smile. Maybe she realized how cold that had sounded? "I'll make good use of your talent."

Thanks?

Turning to Mike and Tom as she settled into her seat, she said, "Gentlemen," and opened a folder in front of her. "What's the update?"

Mike cleared his throat. "Yes. Everything is proceeding as planned. No new suspects have popped up on the radar. Getting McVie and Dalton into place will take us into the final phase before D-day."

"Roles are established?" she asked.

"Yes, though no contact has been made as of yet, other than with Jim. Poppy will be introduced as my girlfriend at the banquet this weekend. I think Dalton should be there, too. The men can meet him, see he's friendly, approachable. Might grease the wheels to getting them interested in a hunt with him."

Hyland nodded, switching her attention to Tom. "How's our mobile business?"

"Sales are good, but all that does is make busy work for me, as you know." He smirked. "Who knew selling taxidermy supplies out of the back of a van could be so lucrative?"

She waited.

"Anyway, as Mike said, no new suspects. Working the same leads. Keeping up the charade." He sounded bored.

He sat back, lifted his coffee mug to his lips.

Ms. Hyland frowned.

Tom sat forward again without having taken a sip, set the mug back down. "I agree that bringing these two in might shake some more rats out of the cellars."

She looked around the table. "Anything else?"

My pulse hummed as my heart rate picked up. "I have something."

All eyes turned to me. Dalton's filled with surprise.

Ms. Hyland stared at me, waiting.

Oh Crap. Wait. She'll want to know how I know. I can't tell her.

"Um." *What was I thinking?* "A friend of mine, just yesterday, happened to go see a party planner." *Oh geez, I didn't think this through.* "You know, a guy who plans children's parties. These real elite shindigs."

Dalton shifted in his chair next to me.

"Well, after he left, the guy called him, my friend I mean, on the phone, and offered him a live snowy owl. For sale as a pet. For a birthday gift. For five grand. For the child."

She stared at me with a blank face. She didn't see the significance.

"This guy is selling live owls. They're popular, you see, because of a character in the Harry Potter books."

"How do you know this?" Ms. Hyland asked.

"Apparently everyone knows but me. Hairwig is his name. Or something like that."

She interlaced her fingers and set her hands on the table. "No. I mean, what makes you confident the story is true?"

"I don't know why my friend would lie."

She shook her head again. "Is there proof there's an actual bird? Was an actual live bird seen? Any confirmation of actual illegal activity?"

"Well, no. Not exactly. But if it is true, he'd have to—"

"But all you have is an offer? And not to you, but a friend? A civilian?"

I nodded. *Damn. This isn't going well.*

"And you brought this to me now because…?" Her eyebrows were up, demanding an answer.

Because the guy hangs out at the taxidermy shop. It can't be a coincidence. But I couldn't say that. "There was just something about the story that bothered me. You know, a gut feeling."

"A gut feeling?" she asked, impatient with me now.

Tom and Mike shifted in their chairs.

"Yes," I said. "This guy could be the retail outlet for a whole trafficking network. I mean, the set up it would take to deliver live snowy owls would be—"

"Exactly." She sounded just like my mom. "That would be quite astounding. The more likely scenario is he's a typical salesman, pulling a bait and switch." She shook her head, blowing me off. "We don't have time for it right now. It's nothing but a distraction." She hesitated, looked back at me. "Unless you have more information you're not telling us?" Her eyes bore into me, expecting an answer.

If I told her, I'd have to explain that I'd followed Hal, and the connection to my friend. I'd have to admit I'd sent Chris, a civilian, to talk to him.

I shrugged. Frustrated. "I can have my friend place the order for the owl, with your permission. See how far he takes it. See if he actually produces the live bird."

"No." She shook her head. "I don't want another minute spent on it." She closed the folder and turned back to Mike. "Let's get this op zipped up. I want that customs leak."

Like that, my case was dismissed.

"Anything else?" she asked, her eyes scanning her team.

All shook their heads.

"This Saturday, I expect you here at oh five hundred. A little team building exercise out at our training center." She rose from the chair. "Don't worry. There'll be time to make it to the banquet that night."

As she turned toward the door, she handed me a slip of paper. "That's the number of a prop shop in town. We have a good relationship with them. Call, ask for Melody. She'll help you dress the part for the banquet. Maybe a fur coat. Whatever."

I took the paper, stared at it as she left the room.

I just told you about a man trafficking in live snowy owls and you're sending me shopping?

"What the hell were you thinking?" Dalton asked once we were out of the building.

"I need more proof. That's all. I should have waited to mention it, yes. Now I just need to get more evidence."

"No. No. No, you don't. And you shouldn't have mentioned it at all. Don't you get it? We're on a team now. The team gets sent on missions. We don't conjure up our own operations. We don't go off investigating every hunch. We focus. We play our part in the bigger arena, to make a bigger impact."

"Well, that doesn't mean we shut off our brains and wear blinders."

"Of course not. But she's right. You have no idea if there's really anything going on there. He could be spouting his mouth off, fishing for sales. Maybe it's his ploy to sell something else. Maybe he gets them pulling the five grand out of their pockets, then says 'oh geez, I just found out it's illegal to own an owl. Who knew? How about this train set instead? It's only four grand.'"

"He's not doing that."

"You don't know that. She's right. You're getting distracted. Haven't you heard that old saying, 'If you chase two rabbits, you won't catch either one'? We haven't been here a week yet." He thrust his hands unto his hips. "I suppose you sent Chris right?"

I didn't answer.

"God, you're incorrigible."

"Incorrigible? Really? That Word-of-the-Day toilet paper is really paying off for you."

"Hey, I'm trying to be your friend here."

"Yeah. Well don't. Go back to rearranging pickles!"

"What?"

"I'll get an Uber back to the shop," I told him as I walked away.

CHAPTER 8

I couldn't punch up Chris's number fast enough.

"Hey. You're not going to believe this. She sent me shopping."

"What? What are you talking about? You told her about the owls, right?"

"Yeah, she thinks he's just running some kind of bait and switch sales thing. Told me not to get distracted. Sent me shopping for a fur coat at some movie prop house. Can you believe it?"

"Well, she might have a point."

"Chris! He's selling owls."

"Okay."

"Dammit."

"What are you going to do about it?"

"I don't know." I thought about it. "What if you call him back and say yes? I mean, tell him you want the owl."

"Are you sure? Wouldn't we have to come up with some money?"

"When did you tell him the birthday party was?"

"Two months from now."

"Damn. That's not going to work."

"Right."

"You can't ask to see the owl, like some kind of confirmation. It would give us away."

"Uh huh."

"If it is a bait and switch thing," I said, "he'd lead you on right up to the day before, so you'd be trapped into his alternative."

"Yep."

"By then, we'll have the poaching sting wrapped up and be shipped out to our next operation."

"Right."

"Crap."

"So what are you going to do?"

"Right now?" I bit my lip. "Go shopping I guess." *Dammit!* "It's over on Halstead. Meet me there?"

"Sure."

I hailed a cab and twenty minutes later I was standing outside an indistinct old warehouse in a questionable neighborhood. I double-checked the address. This was it. I rang the bell.

After two minutes passed, an intercom buzzed to life. "Who's there?"

"Special Agent Poppy McVie for Melody."

"Oh, yes. C'mon in." The door lock clicked open.

A car pulled up and Chris got out. "Just in time."

He followed me in.

In all my travels, I'd never seen such a place. It reminded me of that warehouse in the final scene of *Indiana Jones and the Raiders of the Lost Ark*. Rows and rows of boxes stacked on top of boxes, each aisle labeled with a number.

Melody sat at a dusty desk with a laptop. "What are you looking for?"

"Well, a fur coat for starters," I said, though the thought of actually wearing one made my skin crawl.

"Anything else?"

Chris piped up. "How about a snakeskin belt?"

I shook my head. "A cocktail dress. Shoes, jewelry to go with it. That kind of stuff."

"What are you? About a size four?"

"Give or take."

"Any particular fur?"

"Whatever's most expensive? Mink?"

"Boring," Chris moaned. "Go for chinchilla. Something exotic."

Melody smiled. "I'll see what we've got." She plunked at the computer, then stood up. "Make yourself comfortable. I'll be right back."

"This is pretty slick," Chris said. "Ask and you shall receive."

"Yeah." I wasn't impressed. Who cared about a fur coat when I could be catching an owl trafficker. "Hal is selling live owls. I need more proof, that's all. It would be too hard to find his previous customers. And we can't wait. I need to go on the offensive here. Yes, that's what I need to do. It worked in Costa Rica."

"Are you sure you want to do that? Didn't your boss just tell you to let it go?"

"Yeah, but she doesn't have all the information."

"Neither do you."

"Hey, are you on my side or what?"

"Of course I'm on your side. That's why I'm asking. What if you pursue this only to find out she was right? And you lose your job over it? I mean, the more I think about it, the more I think the odds are, she's right. It'd be a good sales tactic. Sleazy, but I bet it works."

"But my gut tells me there's something more going on."

"Okay. I love you, my dearest Poppy girl. That's why I'm going to say this." He took me by the shoulders and looked me in the eyes. "Maybe your gut just really wants it to be true."

I let my shoulders slump. Could it be?

"Besides, it sounds like you'd have to jump through a lot of hoops to get some proof. You'd have to go behind her back now. You'd be risking a lot. Why? Maybe you should focus on the sting you're assigned to right now."

"God, you sound like Dalton."

"Well, maybe you should listen to him."

I pulled away. "Oh, dammit. Maybe you're right."

Melody was back with several gowns to choose from. I looked to Chris. "Well?"

"This one. For sure," he said, choosing a full-length gold lame dress with a slit all the way up the side.

I took it and headed into the bathroom to try it on. When I emerged, Chris had earrings and a pair of four-inch heels in his hands. "Look at you," he said, his eyebrows dancing.

I moaned.

"You could act like you like fashion for once."

"Yeah, whatever." I eyed the shoes. "I can't outrun a gangster in those."

He shoved them at me. "Wear 'em anyway."

I strapped them to my feet.

Melody came back with a full-length fur coat. "Try this one on," she purred as she slipped it over my shoulders.

"Oooh, weeee," said Chris.

I ran my hands down the front. "Wow, that really is soft."

Then I recoiled. It was my gut that was going soft.

Psychologists call it ruminating. Like cows with their cud. I couldn't let it go. Hal was up to something. And selling owls to rich parents as the ultimate Harry Potter gift made perfect sense. Sure, it might be a sales ploy. But what if it wasn't and we let it slide? Where was the justice for the owls?

And what happens to these owls when the families realize they aren't good pets? What happens to the them then?

Maybe I needed a different tack. I decided to call the local Audubon club, ask if there'd been any sightings in the area this season. There had been. The chapter president, Mr. Anderson, informed me that a snowy was known to hang out down on a long stretch of Lake Michigan beach, and he'd already been spotted there this season. He seemed to know quite a bit about it, and agreed to meet me there. Maybe he'd have some information that would help.

The cold January wind whipped down the shoreline, and cut through my jacket, as I stepped out of the cab. My cheeks burned in the icy chill. But the sun was out, making the snow sparkle like diamonds scattered in the fluff. I drew in a deep breath. Cold or not, it was a respite from the city, and it felt so calming.

Mr. Anderson was already there with a scope set up on a tripod.

I waved. "Thanks for meeting me."

"Any excuse to get out of the house," he said with a warm smile. He took off a fat mitten to shake my hand. "He's been swooping around." He replaced the mitten and adjusted his floppy, hand-knit hat.

"Really?" I scanned the area, hoping to catch a glimpse of the diurnal hunter, with his white plumage and striking yellow eyes. I'd never seen a snowy owl in the wild.

"You'll have to watch for him because you sure won't hear him coming. Owls have silent flight. They're nature's stealth bomber."

"You've seen just this one this season in the Chicago area?" I asked.

"Several people have claimed sightings, but we don't record them unless verified. This guy here is a regular. Comes back nearly every year. The others have been sporadic, in varied locations. No sign of an irruption this year, so that's normal." He scanned with the scope then continued. "Every once in a while, for unknown reasons, snowy owls come flooding down from the arctic in a phenomenon we call an irruption. Most likely it's tied to fluctuations in their food source population, which is mainly lemmings."

I knew quite a bit about owls already, but I didn't want to be rude and cut him off.

"But it's not what you think." He grinned as though he had a great secret. "Irruptions tend to happen when there is an abundance of food at their nesting grounds. The fuller their bellies, it seems, the farther south they fly."

Okay, I didn't know that one. "Interesting," I said. "What else can you tell me?"

"There he is," he said, his voice rising in volume. He pointed and went for the scope.

Along the shoreline, a white bird glided, about ten feet above the ground. To the average onlooker, he could be mistaken for a gull. But those wings didn't flap with urgency, hurried; they moved with a graceful motion, like poetry in the air. This was no scavenger, but a practiced hunter. He tilted those wings, ever so slightly, and glided to a stop atop a large piece of driftwood.

Mr. Anderson adjusted the scope. "There, take a look."

I moved to the scope, shut one eye and peered through the lens. The owl sat perched, his feathers all puffed out and flickering in the breeze, the sun making him seem otherworldly, like a feathered-angel. He turned his head and looked right at me. Those deep yellow eyes caught the sunlight and glowed like topaz. "Oh my God, he's magnificent."

"Amazing creatures. See how he's turning his head, like it's on a swivel? He has to do that to see."

"It looks like he can turn his head nearly all the way around," I said.

"Two hundred and seventy degrees."

"No way."

"Yep. They can't move their eyes within the sockets. They don't have spherical eyeballs like we do. Their eyes are cone-shaped, well, I guess you'd call them elongated tubes, and they're fixed in place. So, they have to turn their heads. They have binocular vision, like a human's, which helps them judge distance for hunting, but the eye shape gives them excellent night vision, too."

The owl blinked, and slowly turned his head in the opposite direction.

"What's really amazing about owls are their ears," he went on, seemingly enjoying having someone interested with which to share his passion. "Some owls have ear tufts, but they're not ears, just display feathers. Their real ears are just openings located at the sides of the head, behind the eyes, where you'd think, but the unique thing is, for most, they're asymmetrically placed. One ear is higher than the other. This helps them hone in on the exact distance of the source of the sound, because the sound waves hit one ear before the other. And if that isn't amazing enough, some owls, such as the barn owl, have a very pronounced facial disc, which acts like a radar dish, guiding sounds into the ear openings. The shape of the disc can be altered at will, using special facial muscles. Isn't that fascinating?"

"It is," I said. But I didn't look up from the scope. The owl was fidgeting, about to take flight again.

He opened his wings and burst into the air, circled out over the ice, then sped northward and out of sight.

Mr. Anderson grinned at me. "What do you think?"

"Absolutely breathtaking."

"Yeah, I never tire of seeing him."

"Have there been any signs of anyone trying to hurt him or capture him?"

His eyebrows scrunched together with concern. "Not that I know of. Why do you ask?"

"Just wondering. Some people are like that."

He nodded, frowning. "I've heard about what some do to eagles. North of here, some were found spray painted and their tail feathers ripped out."

"Yes, unfortunately, I've heard of that, too. Do you know of anyone who keeps owls for pets?"

"No. That's illegal. And they wouldn't make good pets anyway. They're predators." He started to unscrew the scope from its tripod. "There is a raptor rehabilitation center north of the city. They give tours and talks for local kids. If you're interested, I can get you the info."

"Thanks," I said. "I'd appreciate that." There was so much more I wanted to ask. But the bottom line I was getting at, was whether Hal was selling live owls. Mr. Anderson wouldn't know. If he did, he certainly would have reported it.

I bid him goodbye. I had to get back to work.

Back at the shop, I had an email from Greg, the analyst. Some hacker for the bureau, or someone or other, had acquired the guest list for the banquet we were to attend this weekend. I had been assigned the task of running down the list, matching suspects with attendees so Mike and Tom could build the strategy.

Great. More computer time. It didn't get any more boring than this.

But I was doing my part, right?

I started searching folders. Then, half way down the list. There it was. His name. Hal Gruba. He was going to be at the banquet.

You're up to something, buddy, and I'm going to catch you. Or my name isn't Special Agent Poppy McVie.

CHAPTER 9

0500 comes early. We were to report to the downtown office to be transported together from there to the training center, which was somewhere in the outskirts of Chicago.

With one eye open and a mug full of coffee, I piled into the back of an unmarked van with Mike, Tom, and Dalton.

Ms. Hyland had said we'd be doing a team building exercise. I had no idea what to expect. Probably one of those structured "get to know your team" seminars where you build trust, learn to communicate, construct little vessels made of marshmallows and spaghetti to hold an egg, then drop it from a four-story tower, see whose egg doesn't get scrambled.

This was my chance to make an impression. To impress my new boss. I winced. My second chance. Why did Dalton have to be right? I shouldn't have brought up Hal yet. I'd been too excited. I'd jumped the gun. Well, not again. Today would be different.

Glad I didn't have to drive, I pulled my coat collar up around my neck, snugged it tightly, and lay my head back to rest my eyes. With the banquet tonight, it was going to be a long day.

We arrived at the training center in the dark. In fact, this time of year, the sun wouldn't be up for at least another hour.

"We'll be training outside today," Ms. Hyland said as we entered the building. "Gear up. Garb's in the locker rooms."

I followed Ms. Hyland into the ladies' locker room. We were

the only women here.

She handed me a white snowsuit and took one for herself.

"Are you training with us?" I asked, surprised.

"You never stop learning or needing practice," she said.

"Right."

"In the main hall, you'll get your headgear," she said, donning the suit, then left the room without another word to me.

Headgear? I zipped up my suit and followed her out.

Dalton, Tom, and Mike were already there, sorting through a bin of helmets and face shields.

"What are we doing exactly?" I asked.

Dalton gave me a wink. What did he know that I didn't?

As soon as we all had our appropriately-fitting headgear, Ms. Hyland told us to follow her.

In the next room, an over-sized closet really, were rows of weapons. Paint-ball guns. There were long-barreled sniper rifles, traditional pump-action rifles, semi-automatics, and pistols.

"You each get a sidearm and your choice of long gun. Choose your best weapons. They may seem like toys, but they're not the kind you'd pick up at Walmart. These semi-automatics fire as fast as the real deal, but the pump-action models are more accurate."

Other people started to arrive in the building. "We share this facility with the state police, as well as other federal law enforcement agencies," she explained. "A lot of other players will be joining us this morning." She stood erect. "This is an elite team. Let's act like one. You have fifteen minutes to sight in your weapon of choice."

The four of us quickly grabbed our weapons. I chose a pump-action. Guns never interested me, though, in my training as a field agent, I was required to become proficient with their use, and, by some form of irony, I'd aced weapons training in school. Top of my class, actually. Shooting targets is fun, but I'd hoped I could avoid ever aiming a weapon at a person or an animal. Unfortunately, I'd learned that lesson the hard way, though. Sometimes, in this profession, you have no choice.

We headed to the outdoor range. I was surprised at how accurate these toy guns really were. Other than the big ammunition hopper on the top, they felt and handled more like the real deal than I would have thought. The pistols held a six round magazine, of which we had one. If we used those six rounds, we would have to reload by hand.

Once we were geared up, weapons ready, we gathered for a rules briefing. The head of the training center—a heavily-muscled, bald guy with a commanding baritone—explained how the games were played.

Today, we'd be engaged in a version of woodsball. There would be two teams per round. Each had a flag to place wherever they saw fit within their half of the playing grounds, as long as it was visible from at least 270 degrees and no more than ten feet off the ground. The object was to retrieve the enemy flag, and carry it safely to your own flag's location for the win.

It was elimination play. If I got shot, I was out.

No aiming at the head. In fact, they were so adamant about it, if a player got shot in the head, not only did the shot not count, but the shooter, if caught, was ejected.

Also, if in close range, saying bang was the preferred method to take out a competitor. Apparently, being shot by a paintball from a few feet away hurts like hell, and if you're good enough to get that close undetected, you don't have to waste the ammo.

Our playing ground was an eighty-acre patch of woods— mostly pines, a few oaks, a valley of scrub brush—and some man-made obstacles like blinds and towers.

"We're playing in the first round," Ms. Hyland said. She gestured toward me. "Poppy and Mike, you'll be on one team, Dalton, Tom and I on the other."

"We're not one team?" Tom asked.

"No." She gave no other explanation. That meant we were teamed with people we didn't know. Was that the point? See how we worked with strangers?

A bell rang, alerting us to get on the field into position.

Dalton hung back as the others dispersed, looking at me.

"Have fun," he said. "And may the best man win." He winked.

He was goading me. "Yes, good luck to you," I said, turning away, unwilling to give him any satisfaction.

My team consisted of Mike and me, two state police officers, one Chicago city cop, and a conservation officer from downstate Illinois. We huddled for a quick strategy session near the border on our end.

Mike took the initiative to lead the conversation. "I'm thinking we take roles like a hockey team. What do you think? Three on offense. Two hang back. And the goalie." The other men were nodding. "Anyone interested in defense?"

The conservation officer took the fluorescent orange flag from him. "Sure, I'll goal tend."

"You could just tuck it in your pocket," Mike said.

The guy frowned. "I don't think that's legal."

"Yeah, of course not," Mike said. "Just testing you."

The city cop, Mike, and I were to be on offense. "Our job," Mike said, "is to take out the enemy and get their flag."

"Good plan," I said. "And the strategy?"

"Shoot anything that moves," he said with a chuckle and turned toward the opposing side, ready to go. The others dispersed to take their positions.

That was it? I got that this was a training exercise, team building. But Mike seemed pretty laid back about it. Our boss was here. Shouldn't we give it our best?

When our other teammates were out of earshot, I said, "It seems like a pretty loose strategy. I wonder if we should—"

He smirked. "It's a game. Loosen up. Have some fun."

I guess.

The temperature was in the mid-20s, with a light breeze. Heavy snow lined the tree limbs and there was a good base on the ground, though this area had been so heavily used the day before, tracking would be nearly impossible. Footprints covered the ground everywhere.

The terrain was rolling, heavily wooded in most of the area, with a few open spots. I headed for a patch of pines. Their boughs drooped to the ground, snow-laden. It seemed a good spot for cover as I worked my way to the opposing side to find the flag.

A siren blew and the game officially began.

I chose to move up the edge of the playing field, so I only had a hundred and eighty degrees to watch. It was a solid strategy for now, but the flag wouldn't be hanging on the fence. I'd eventually have to move inward.

I moved at a crouch, keeping low, scanning the area, my rifle out in front of me.

Mike kept with me. "Don't you think we should split up?" I asked when I stopped to hunker down and assess the area.

"No. This way we can cover each other," he said. "You know, give back up. Like partners."

"Oh-kay," I said. What was that supposed to mean? I'd already asked for a strategy and he gave none. Now he wanted to proceed like partners?

"We need to move through those pines," I said, nodding toward a thick stand. "See what's on the other side."

"Good idea," he said with a wink.

Down on my belly, I crawled through the snow on my elbows, slowly, carefully placing each elbow and knee, my rifle at the ready. Mike followed on my heels.

When I came to a halt to assess the area beyond, he crawled up beside me. "We won't be able to see the flag if we stay on the ground."

"What are you suggesting?"

"One of us has to stand up at some time."

I glanced upward. "I could climb a tree to get a look around."

"Are you serious?"

"Except I'd probably get shot."

"They say, no one thinks to look up."

"Yeah, if they were directly below me. But from a distance…"

"Alls I know is, the intel would be priceless."

He was right. Half the battle was getting close enough to find their flag. If I could see it from here, we'd be golden.

"Go find an angle where you can cover me," I said.

"Right on." And he slithered away through the snow.

I couldn't hold my rifle and climb. I'd be defenseless. Sure, I could flip it over my back, and I also had my sidearm strapped to my thigh. But shinnying up a tree was risky. Mike was right, though, the intel would be worth it.

I'd be quick about it. Then right back down.

I leaned my rifle against the trunk of the tree, grabbed hold of a branch, pulled upward, grabbed the next branch, then the next, and I was fifteen feet up. The woods were thick, but that yellow fluorescent flag stood out like a beacon. A quick compass read showed 325 degrees.

I descended as fast as I could, grabbed my weapon, and followed Mike's trail in the snow.

"I found it," I said, pretty happy with myself. We'd barely started the game. "Follow me."

"Right behind you," I heard him say, without any sarcasm.

The odds were, the other team would have a similar strategy as ours. They'd have one person dedicated to protecting the flag, probably a line of defense somewhere not far from the flag, and an aggressive offense.

As we closed in on our prize, Mike came up beside me. "I see their flag tender," he whispered. "He's got his back against that tree."

"Just one? We haven't seen another player." That didn't

seem likely. "Where are the others?"

"I don't see anyone else. They probably went aggressive and put them all on offense. We need to act fast, before they get our flag and get back here."

"Yeah, but—"

"This is our chance. The longer we wait, the more we lose the advantage."

"Good point," I said. But still, there didn't seem to be—

"The moment we take him out, we sprint for the flag. Before the others know what happened."

It wasn't a bad idea. Risky, but it could work.

"I bet you're a fast runner. I mean, you're in such great shape, by the way." He gave me a conspiratorial grin. "I'll take him out and you run. Deal?"

"Deal," I said, grinning back. "Let me get into position."

"Roger that," he said and put his rifle to his shoulder.

I sneaked past a scotch pine, then found a good, protected hiding spot from which to launch into a sprint. With my rifle slung securely over my shoulder, I nodded to Mike.

He nodded confirmation, lined up his target, and fired.

The moment I saw the paint splat on that white suit I was running, straight for that flag. It was several feet up the tree. I'd have to jump, grab a branch, and haul myself up to reach it. I'd be quick, then run for cover.

A few more strides. One, two, three. The branch was there. I reached, pulled. The flag was right there.

"Bang!"

What?

"Bang!"

I dropped to the ground, looked around.

"Got you." Dalton's voice. *Dammit!*

But where was he?

Then I saw it. An area where the snow had been disturbed, ever so slightly more than the snow around. Twigs and branches lay atop the snow there. When I looked closer, there he was.

His eyes. He'd buried himself in the snow, lying in wait.

Dammit, dammit, dammit! I should have known. I should have anticipated this. I should have seen it.

I held my hands above my head, the signal that I'd been ejected from the game, and headed for the building with my tail between my legs.

What had I been thinking? Here I was trying to impress Ms. Hyland and I couldn't keep my head on straight. *Dammit!*

After seven more rounds of woodsball, where I sat on the sidelines, watching, I slinked back to the van and kept my head down all the way back into the city.

CHAPTER 10

"Don't be mad at me," Dalton whispered in my ear, the first moment we were alone. He was trying to get me to flirt.

We were standing on the corner, two blocks from the downtown office. After we'd returned from the training center, I'd made a lame excuse about wanting to run an errand before getting ready for the banquet tonight. I needed time to think, alone. Then Dalton had glommed onto me.

"Why would I be mad at you?" I said, trying not to snarl. "You got me. Fair and square."

He frowned. I was right. What could he say?

"I should have thought it through. It seemed too good to be true and it was."

He stared at me, waiting for more.

I shifted my weight to the other foot. "It was just a game."

A nod. But he and I both knew that the traits and skills used in a game like that were the same that would play out in real-life situations.

"You're right," he said. "It was just a game. You wanted to win. You let that go to your head is all. Rookie mistake."

Every muscle of mine seized up, holding in my frustration. I managed a shrug. "You're right."

"What?" He pulled back, a look of surprise on his face. "You're not going to deny it? You're not going to argue? You're obviously an imposter. What have you done with the real Poppy?"

I shrugged again. Why couldn't he let this go? "There's nothing to argue. You're right. You know I'm not a great team player."

"Listen," he said, taking my hand. "Being on this team is going to be an adjustment. For both of us. But it's what you wanted, remember?"

"I guess." Ugh. I couldn't talk about this right now.

"You've already changed your mind?"

"No. I just..." I yanked my hand from his and crossed my arms.

"What is it? What's gotten into you?"

"Nothing." *Just leave me alone to be angry with myself for a while. Geez.*

"C'mon. This is me you're talking to." He gave me those lusty eyes. "Your Dalton."

"My Dalton?" I said, my head spinning now. "Who are you? To me? What is this anyway? Between us? I don't even... we haven't even..."

He cocked his head to the side. "Is that what's bothering you?"

"No. Yes. I don't know." *Ohmigod. Go away!*

"Well, I didn't want to put any added pressure on...things."

"What are you talking about? I thought you and I, and that we, but you..."

"Now what are you talking about?"

I covered my eyes with my hands. "I can't do this right now."

"Exactly," he said. "We need to focus. You need to be able to focus on the job without unnecessary distractions."

My head snapped up. "Unnecessary distractions? Is that what I am, a distraction?"

"No, that's not what I—"

"So, you made that decision? About us? Without asking me how I feel about it?"

"Well, I—"

I spun around and headed across the street.

He ran after me. "Poppy, c'mon. Talk to me."

I reeled around to face him. "Why didn't you tell me you'd already met Mike and Tom. Why'd you lie?"

"Wait a minute. I didn't lie." He looked down the street, shoved his hands in his jeans pockets, then looked back to me. "I just didn't mention it."

"Purposefully didn't mention it. Why?"

"Because they asked me not to. They were curious, that's all. They asked me all about you, what to expect."

"Yeah, well, they didn't ask me all about you."

His eyes shot from one side to the other and he blew out a breath. "They figured since you're an admiral's kid and all that—"

My mouth dropped open. "How could they find that out? Our personal information is supposed to be—"

"They knew. And they assumed you'd be a pain in the ass. Had a chip on their shoulders about it, actually. I thought,"—his hand shot up, gesturing toward me—"and I was right, that you'd be upset about it. So, I thought it was best not to mention it."

"And you told them I've earned my place on the team? That I'm a good agent and—"

He frowned. "What do you think?"

I sighed. "So, that had nothing to do with, with why you and I aren't—"

"No."

I crossed my arms. "It was my mom, wasn't it. Showing up like that. Because she can. She got to you."

He curled up his lip. "What? No."

"I know how she is."

His hands landed on his hips. "I'm a SEAL, for God's sake. I'm not afraid of your mom."

A giggle burst from me. I had no idea why or where it came from. But this was insane. "Distraction? Really, that's the best you could come up with? What we have—*had*—was a distraction?"

He looked hurt. "That's not what I said. That's not what I meant. But, Jesus, Poppy, you want to talk about distractions? What the hell was all that about the guy selling owls? You sent Chris? What were you thinking? You need to forget about that."

"You said yourself that he was odd."

"I didn't say to send Chris after him."

"Yeah, well. Thanks for the support," I said and spun back around and headed down the block.

"Poppy, what is wrong with you?" he shouted after me.

"I can't talk now! I saw something shiny!"

The woman in the mirror stared back at me, standing there in that dreadful fur coat. Her red hair sprang out all over the place. Her face looked sad, forlorn.

"You yelled at Dalton. You acted like a spoiled brat. If he wasn't done with you before, he is now."

The sad face turned into a frown.

Mike's voice blared through the intercom speaker. "You ready to go?"

I walked to the intercom, held the button, "Yep, I'll be right down."

Back at the mirror, I gave the reflection an encouraging smile. "Perk up there, sassy. You're going to a fancy wild game banquet with your rich boyfriend."

Ugh. Method acting. No conjuring of character would make me eat meat. Or forget about Dalton. I'd figure it out when I got there. I also needed to figure out how in the world I was going to get Mike to invite Hal to his guys' party without grilling me for reasons.

I tried it one more time; I adjusted my posture and winked at my image in the mirror. "You'll think of something."

The movie star had even left the keys to his car. Mike pulled it from the garage. Some kind of foreign, sporty, kind of thing. Mike seemed impressed, so I guess it must have been impressive.

I got in the passenger seat and we sped out of the driveway.

The banquet was being held at a local sportsmen club. After dinner, there'd be a live auction, then cocktails and lots of bragging. Mike would turn on the charm.

"Do me a favor. Don't take too much food on your plate," I told him as he shoved his foot down on the gas pedal. "You might have to eat mine."

He turned to look at me, eyebrows up. "What? Why?"

"Eyes on the road."

He frowned, turned back.

"It's wild game, right? I'm a vegetarian."

His eyes swung back around and landed on me. "You can't be serious."

"Eyes on the road!"

He kept his eyes glued to me as he downshifted and gunned it.

I gave him a smile. "It'll be fine. And I love wine, so I won't embarrass you there. Fashion sense, on the other hand...well, let's hope it doesn't come up."

"Do I need to ask?"

"Nope."

Mike seemed deep in thought about that the rest of the drive.

The club was a chalet-style hall overlooking a pond surrounded by acres of woods. The full moon cast a bluish glow on the snow. Oh, for a pair of snowshoes and a fuzzy hat. But no, my job tonight was to hobnob with a bunch of blowhards whose favorite hobby was to kill big animals, the more rare and exotic, the better.

Mike drove right up to the front entrance to use the valet, of course.

We strode in, arm in arm—like royalty. Mike had timed our arrival so we would be a little late, so everyone in attendance would see us walk in. He really did know how to do this job well.

I scanned the room for Hal, but I didn't see him anywhere.

Dalton leaned against the bar, a Manhattan in his hand. He seemed out of place. But, I suppose, that was because I knew the real Dalton. Kind, strong, committed. No pretense there.

Jim chatted with a group of men. One I recognized as Frank Lutz, our main target. It made me wonder if we could truly trust Jim. He seemed like a genuine man, but how much effort had been put in to vetting him?

A woman approached Jim, one of the wives I assumed, and gave him a hug, her expression somber. Condolences for the loss of his wife.

Mike gave me a nudge. I smiled and turned so he could lift my coat from my shoulders and hand it in for coat check. He made a big show of it.

"You look stunning tonight, my darling," he said and gave me a quick kiss on the lips.

Wasn't expecting that. But then again, he was supposed to be making me known. He took me by the hand and led me into the crowd.

The way he commanded attention, the way he owned the room, was impressive. I had to admit, Mike was damn good at playing the arrogant, hunting-obsessed rich guy. If I hadn't known better, I'd have believed every word he said. That he had a talent for method acting was an understatement. I had some things to learn from this man. Not only did he play the part well, he had the ability to make the other men feel at ease, to trust him. You can't teach that stuff.

With his personality, he truly was in the right role for this operation. Or maybe he was exceptionally adaptable. Was he this good in other roles? I'd be curious to see.

After we worked half the room, he strode right over to Frank, thrust his hand out and pumped the man's arm. Then he wrapped his arm around my waist and yanked me toward him, nearly knocking me off my heels.

"This here's my girl, Poppy."

Frank shook my hand while giving me the once-over with a nod of approval, as though I were a new car or a trophy mount.

I gave him my yeah-I'm-hot-stuff-there-big-boy grin.

"Tuesday night. My place," Mike said. It wasn't a question. "Some bourbon, cigars."

Frank nodded, as though there were some conspiratorial thing among men. No more explanation was needed.

"I want to introduce my guide around. So, bring along some friends." He winked. "Friends with discretion, of course."

Frank nodded some more, all in.

It felt too easy. But I knew, Mike had spent months establishing his character, knowing these men would respond this way. It was something to witness.

"Babe, why don't you go get us some drinks," he said to me. "Bring me a bourbon. On the rocks."

"Sure thing."

He patted me on the butt when I turned and I heard him say, "She was a waitress when I met her." Would have been nice if I'd known that little bit of info.

I headed toward the bar, the walk on those heels a balancing act, and nearly tripped when I saw Hal. He was here. Standing right next to Dalton, his hand wrapped around a bottle of Bud Lite.

I approached. "Well, hello there," I said with a big smile. "I see you took my advice."

Blank face. He didn't remember me. Really? With this crazy hair?

"I work at Wilson's Taxidermy shop. Didn't you come in a few days ago?"

"Oh, yeah. Yeah. I didn't know you were Mike's girlfriend." His eyes lit up like I was some kind of celebrity.

Hm. Well, this could be useful.

Aloof, I turned to the bartender. "Bourbon on the rocks and do you have a wine list?"

"We have two. Red or white," the bartender said with a smirk.

"Ah," I said. "I'll have the house red."

That got me a gracious nod.

"So, how do you know Mike?" I asked, turning back, acting as if I wasn't really interested, but had to be polite.

With a dopey shrug, he said, "Everyone knows Mike."

Right.

I grinned. The way to get Hal to Mike's party was too obvious. A *faux pax*. I had to commit a *faux pax*.

"Have you met Dalton?" I said, gesturing in his direction. "A good friend of Mike's."

Hal turned to meet Dalton.

"I'm sure you'll hear all about him at the party Tuesday night," I added.

Hal paused, looked at me quizzically.

I acted as though I were hiding my mistake. "Or…some other time."

Dalton flashed me a look of warning. He knew what I was up to.

My wine was poured. I picked up the glass, took a sip. The ice cubes clinked in the glass as the bartender set the bourbon down. I snatched it up, spun around, and headed for Mike, leaving Dalton to chat with Hal. I'd set the hook.

Guests were asked to be seated. Dinner was served. I managed to get away with a plate of salad and pasta. Nobody noticed.

The live auction bored me into a stupor. I smiled and nodded like a good girlfriend while Mike bid on everything, but won nothing. How he managed to pull that off was beyond me.

Finally, we could get up from the chairs and mingle again. Hal was still hanging around. In fact, he was looking my way, watching. Now I needed to get Mike on board, to get him to invite Hal to his private party.

First, I had to get Mike away from Dalton. The two were

working the room, Mike making introductions, Dalton charming them into wanting his guide service. Just as they'd planned.

I brought Mike another drink. "Honey, can I talk to you for a minute?" I asked, tugging on his arm.

He excused himself and followed me to a corner.

"I need for you to do something," I said.

"Anything for you, darling."

"Cute," I said. "No one can hear us right now."

He nuzzled my cheek. "Anything for you."

Okay. "There's a man over there. Blue shirt, skinny tie. See him?"

"I think so."

"Hal Gruba is his name. He comes into the shop a lot. Never buys. I think he's up to something."

"Like what?"

"I can't go into it all right now. But—" *please* "—trust me, we should keep an eye on him. Invite him to the party."

He pulled away from me, shaking his head. "That would be awkward. I've never seen him before. He doesn't know me."

C'mon. "Well, that's just it. He does know you. This larger-than-life character you've got going has gotten attention. And I've already set the stage for it. When I introduced him to Dalton, I made like I slipped up, as though I'd assumed he was invited. All you have to do is fix your girlfriend's *faux pax*."

He stared at me for a long moment, his eyes scrutinizing me. Was he impressed that I'd thought of that? Or annoyed with me? I couldn't tell.

"He's infatuated with the idea of big game hunting," I added, filling the silence. "Just introduce yourself, then act all flattered or whatever. You'll think of something. If anyone can, you can. You're a pro at this."

"Well, there is that," he said with a wink. "Anything for you, babe."

Another kiss and he merged back into the crowd.

Really? That was it? He'd do it? Well, that was easy. Okay then.

Soon, Mike made his way to Hal and engaged him in conversation. Heads nodded. Then it was time to leave.

After all the goodbyes, all the hand shaking and the so-nice-to-meet-yous, we were finally back in the car.

"So, you invited Hal?" I asked, trying not to sound anxious. "Did he say he'd come?"

Mike grinned. "He was downright giddy."

Great. *Great.*

"Are you going to tell me why?"

"Gut feeling. I tell you what. I'll explain everything after the party. Okay?"

He shrugged. "Sure."

No lecture? No interrogation? Well, that was refreshing. I could get used to a partner like this.

CHAPTER 11

Tonight was the night. It was now or never. I had to get the goods on Hal—some specifics, something—if I were to have a chance at all of nailing this guy.

First things first. I needed to get Hal alone. Should be easy enough.

The bar was stocked. Cigars put out. Cards on the table.

By 8:00 p.m., the men would be here, guzzling drinks, swapping hunting stories, doing what men do.

Mike reminded me that my role was to hang around, act the clingy girlfriend, be an extra set of eyes. "You should take a position of unimportance," he said. Whatever that meant. "You know, so you can observe."

Right. I could do that. And figure out Hal.

At seven forty-five, the first car rolled up. Then, one right after another, all the guests arrived, including Hal. Fifteen men plus Mike and Dalton.

Before the last guest arrived, I swear, Mike called me honey-bunny forty times. Normally, that would annoy the crap out of me, but somehow, it seemed affectionate. Maybe I was adapting to his method-acting technique. Or maybe I was enjoying that tiny, almost imperceptible flinch on Dalton's face every time Mike said it.

Glasses clinked with ice cubes, cigars were lit, and a whole lot of testosterone-induced bragging ensued while the men stood around the trophy display. I loitered on the sidelines, eyes open.

Frank had the biggest mouth, which was amusing to me, considering he was a dentist. He didn't seem worried one bit about the possibility of cops in attendance. Probably thought he was above the law anyway. Made sense, I suppose. When all it takes to bag your own illegal species, without any other penalty, is a big roll of cash. And he seemed to have a lot of it.

As the reports had indicated, Eric, Larry, and Mark hung by his side, sputtering vague stories of their own. Nothing specific I could note. Their files contained long sheets on their poor treatment of women, though they made no rude comments to me. Not even a lear. Perhaps that was a honor-among-men thing. I was, after all, Mike's babe.

Other than the god-awful cigar smoke (had the movie star approved cigar smoking in the house?), the party was rather benign. Boring actually. Why did men like these find this so appealing?

At some point, once enough alcohol had been consumed, Mike would address the whole group. He'd make the pitch to join him and Dalton on a hunt, one that would blow their minds, cash only, of course. That would get them chattering like hens.

That's when I'd make my move. They'd be mingling, asking questions, discussing details. My plan was to lure Hal to the secret trophy room. Then I'd, well, then I'd figure out what to do. The one thing I knew about him was his infatuation with the exotic mounts. I'd run with that.

Meanwhile, I did my job. Kept my eyes open. I had to admit, from my position of utter unimportance, as Mike had put it, I did have a unique opportunity to witness some interesting behavior.

When Mike excused himself from a conversation and went to the bar to refill his drink, I motioned for him to follow me into the kitchen.

"I noticed Frank's friend, Tommy, seemed to be a little uncomfortable," I said. "When you were telling the story about bagging the cheetah, he—"

"Rocked back and forth on his heels. I know. It's a nervous twitch. He's not a target. In fact, I wouldn't be surprised if the agency gets an anonymous tip about me." He grinned as though it would be a point of pride if it happened.

"Okay. I also noticed that Larry's side kick, Eric, seems more interested in—"

"Drinking my scotch? Yes. Classic mooch."

"Right," I said.

"Anything else?"

I shook my head. "I guess I *am* utterly unimportant."

"Yeah, you're doing great," he said, and left me in the kitchen.

Great.

As I headed for the door, Dalton came in.

"What's up?" he asked.

"Nothing," I said.

"Nothing? Are you sure? I thought maybe you had some intel, *honey bunny.*"

"Driving you crazy, isn't it?"

"Right to the nut house." He grinned. "Actually, if anything's driving me crazy, it's that dress."

"This old thing?"

"Well, it's not so much the dress, but the way it shows the skin, right here." He slid his hand from my neck over the spaghetti strap and down my shoulder.

"Yeah? Sorry, tonight this shoulder belongs to Mike."

In true Dalton style, he just shook his head no.

"And this freckle on the back of your neck." He drew his fingers down my neck, ever so lightly, making me shiver.

I tried unsuccessfully to ignore how this kitchen seemed to be heating up. "Yep, as a matter of fact," I managed, "I may have to march out there right now and give him a big, sloppy kiss. How would you like that?"

"I'd have to challenge him to a duel, a fight to the death." He stepped closer, put his lips to my ear. "Because I must have you for my own."

A giggle escaped my lips. "And how do we explain you being in here with me now?"

He pulled away. "Oh, that. I had a hankering for a cup of coffee. So, brew up a pot, would ya?" With a wink, he turned and left.

"I guess I have to make a pot a coffee," I said to no one, catching my breath.

After another hour of small talk, Mike got everyone's attention. "Well, I see no one's willing to play poker. Afraid I'll take all your money?" he said, with a chuckle. "Let's get right down to it. Let's talk hunting."

He gestured toward Dalton. "As you know, I invited all of you tonight to have a chance to meet my man, Dalton, here. I can't begin to tell you what a phenomenal guide he's been. I wouldn't hire anyone else. Not only is he the best in the business for tracking big game, discretion is his middle name, if you know what I mean."

Seemed to me he was laying it on a bit thick, but the men were licking it up.

Hal was the only one who wasn't smiling and nodding. He seemed more interested in the pretzel dip than the hunting expeditions. He fit into this crowd like a coyote trying to hang out with a pack of wolves. This guy didn't make any sense.

Mike went on. "Not only has he helped me bag just about every animal in this room, he had my back while he was doing it. In fact, the last time we were out—" He paused. "You know what, I need to shut up and let him tell the story." He slapped Dalton on the back. "Go on."

"Thanks, man," Dalton said. "Yeah, well, we was up in Alaska, huntin' bear. We'd been dropped off in a really remote area, a spot where I'd seen this big boy ambling through for weeks. I got my man, Mike here, all set up, in a beautiful spot, and—"

"It was, too," Mike added.

Dalton nodded. "Nice angle on the game trail. It was all a matter of luring him in. But the first day, the sumbitch wasn't anywhere in sight. I thought Mike'd fire me for sure."

"Naw," Mike said.

"Well, second day out, I knew I had to find him. So, I got Mike all situated again and I set off cross-country. I found him all right. Got him worked up and running—"

"How'd you do that?" one of the men asked.

Dalton grinned. "Trade secret." That was code for illegal.

He meant a drone. Dalton was using our recent experience with a bear poacher we'd gone undercover to bust in Alaska as his example. Smart. He really was good at this, too—playing the part, making it believable. And who wouldn't be drawn to him, with his charming smile and trustworthy way about him.

Oh man. I've fallen hard.

"Well," Dalton went on. "I'm running toward Mike, hollering for him to get ready, the bear's a comin' and, uh." He paused.

"It's all right. You can tell them," Mike said. "It was a warm, sunny day. And well—"

"There he was," Dalton took back over, "leaning up against a rock, sound asleep." That got him a few laughs. "I shouted as loudly as I could. When he came around, he jumped to his feet like his ass was on fire, gun in hand. By that time, that bear was coming over the ridge, right at him, with a vengeance.

"Mike played it cool though. Waited till that griz was fifty yards away and dropped him with one shot. I ain't seen nothing like it."

Smooth. Dalton was showing how he'd make his hunter look good, no matter what. That part was where the story varied from our real experience, that was for sure.

"My favorite hunt with Mike, though, was in Tanzania, about—" he turned to Mike "—what year was that?"

"Hell, I don't know. What's it matter?" Mike said.

They were having fun batting back and forth.

"You're right. Anyway, Mike here wanted a cheetah." He went on to spin a tall tale. He knew there was a cheetah upstairs as well as all the other animals. He could go on like this all night.

Finally, when he had the men thoroughly enthralled, he segued into the pitch for an upcoming hunt. He was good. Really good. He made a soft sell. Nothing too forward, encouraging them to ask questions.

The men were served more drinks and stood around shooting the shit, taking turns talking with Dalton and Mike, asking for details.

Hal hovered over the bar, munching on peanuts. It was time.

"I get the feeling hunting's not really your thing," I said in a low whisper.

He didn't acknowledge one way or the other.

"But big money is."

That got his attention. "I beg your pardon?"

"Don't worry. Your secret's safe with me. Who wouldn't want to get in here to see that award-winning display?" I nodded toward the bear in the tree. "It's a work of art."

He gave me a polite smile. "Indeed."

"Would you like to see something truly exotic?" I asked him, keeping my voice down.

"What do you mean?"

"Well, when you came in the shop, you seemed really into the more rare animals. And—" I lowered my voice even more to sound like I didn't want anyone else to know "—Mike has this secret room. You won't believe what he's got in there."

His eyes lit up. "Yeah? Like what?"

Gotcha. "I can sneak you up there right now."

"Yeah. No. I dunno." He shook his head, dropped his eyes, and poked around in the peanut bowl some more. "Maybe if

Mike goes."

Well, that won't work. "Oh, I don't know if he will. I mean, tonight. It's uh, called the secret room for a reason, if you know what I mean. But trust me. He won't mind. He loves to show it off." I paused for effect. "To people he trusts."

His attention was still on Mike. What was it about Mike?

Fine. Another tactic. "Are you interested in hunting with Mike some time? That deal they're offering seems like a great opportunity."

He shrugged. "Yeah, I dunno."

What is it with this guy? "I don't know why, but Mike is obsessed with those hunts. He has to do them all the time."

Hal's eyes traveled around the huge room. "Well, he's earned it." His thoughts seemed to take him away for a long moment, then he turned to engage me, finally, like a light switch had flipped on and he'd realized I might be useful. "You know, I've been rude," he said, turning on the salesman charm. "Tell me about your job. Are you studying to be a taxidermist yourself?"

I grinned. Finally some barrier had been broken through. Wish I knew what it was. "Yeah, yeah. Jim has been kind to take me on as an apprentice." He'd mentioned birds. "I'm really interested in birds though, and Jim doesn't do birds."

"Oh, that's too bad."

"You're a bird hunter, right?"

"Oh, not a hunter really. I mean, not like Mike." He took a sip of his drink. "How well do you know him? How long have you been together?"

Back to Mike. Okay. "For years. Well, actually," I said it like an admission, "we have this on-again-off-again thing going on. But really, I can't help it. I love him, you know." I was going to have to wash my mouth out with soap.

He nodded, seemed to accept that answer. "You know, now that I think about it, I would like to see that room."

"Yeah, sure," I said, surprised. *That was too easy. What was he up to?* "Follow me." I turned and headed for the stairs before he could change his mind, hoping he was right behind me.

He was.

At the top of the stairs, I beelined for the room. With my hand on the doorknob, it hit me. The money. Hal was interested in Mike's money. But why? Certainly he'd made himself too obvious if he planned to rob him. No. That wasn't it. He was trafficking in illegal birds. A sales gig. Was he looking for an investor? Is that why he'd stopped in the taxidermy shop so many times? Hoping to meet someone with deep pockets who saw the potential in animals for sale? Someone with questionable business practices? At least that explained his behavior.

I pushed the door open.

Hal followed me in and came to a halt, his mouth agape as he took in the elephant standing in the center of the room.

"I know. Isn't it magnificent?" I said.

"How'd he get that in here?"

"He had the house built around it. Look at that polar bear. It's my favorite. Talk about exotic. Whew."

"Yeah." He slowly moved around the room, his eyes lingering on one animal at a time, asking me questions about the hunt, questions I couldn't possibly have the answer to, before moving to the next. For a guy who didn't seem interested in hunting, he sure was enamored with the kill.

Either way, I didn't have time for this. If the money was the key, I had to work it.

"He truly loves his trophies. You'd be surprised," I said, "at how lucrative the taxidermy business can be. That's why I'm buying Wilson's."

That got his attention. "Are you?"

"Yeah. I'll be honest. I'm not that interested in taxidermy for its own sake. I mean, I'll hire someone to do that work when Jim retires. It's the potential in the numbers. You see, it's all about positioning in the market. The sky's the limit, you know, on what these hunters are willing to pay. I plan to leverage Jim's current clientele with—" I frowned. "I'm sorry. This business talk probably bores you."

"No, not at all. Please go on."

"Well, if we can get some awards, for the work, we can charge a lot more. And then there's…" I let the words trail off, giving him the impression I felt I'd said too much.

"Then there's what?"

"You know, on second thought, I'm not sure I should have brought you up here. Mike has some special mounts that I shouldn't share."

"I'm not going to tell anyone."

"Yes, well." I headed for the door, hoping he'd take the bait. "Maybe some other time, maybe it will work out for Mike to show you himself."

He made no move to follow. "Wow, even a bald eagle," he said, eyeing the mount hanging over the door.

I spun around.

He grinned. "I'm pretty sure it's illegal to have a bald eagle."

"Shit! You're a cop," I said, an age-old trick to gain his trust.

His eyes snapped to mine. "What?"

"And I just walked you right in here," I said, adding fear to my voice. "Oh my god, I'm such an idiot."

He held up a hand. "No, I—"

"That's why you stop in the shop all the time. Jim said you never buy anything. You're trying to catch him at something."

"No, no," he shook his head. "Don't worry. I'm not a cop."

"Yeah, that's just what a cop would say."

He held up his hands. "No, really. I swear it."

"Okay, I believe you," I said, as though I did not believe him. "Let's get back downstairs."

"I'm not a cop, okay."

"Okay. Still, let's get back downstairs." I waited. Had I blown it? He'd either tell me now, not wanting to lose the connection to Mike, or it was over and I'd lost him.

"I've just—" He clammed up.

"Just what?"

"I've been hoping to meet someone like Mike, someone who would be—"

Say it!

"I've just been looking for an investor, the right investor."

Yes! "Investor?" I said with surprise and a hint of intrigue. Ha! So that *was* it.

His jaw tightened. "You're sharp. I bet you'll make a killing at the taxidermy shop. Through the front door"—he gave me a wink—"and the back."

I started to shake my head.

"Don't worry," he said. "I think it's brilliant. You'll probably pocket some serious coin on that endeavor. Just be careful."

I smiled, acting as though I was trying not to acknowledge what I'd been up to.

"I have a similarly lucrative yet *sensitive* business in the works."

"That's what you want Mike to invest in?"

He nodded. "I've been hoping to get a chance to talk with him. He seems like an entrepreneurial kind of guy. Would you say so?"

Now that I had him back, I didn't like where this was going. I had to convince him I'd be a good partner and keep Mike out of this. I couldn't involve my teammates until I had irrefutable evidence and I couldn't take the case back to my boss without it. "Yeah. If it's the right thing. A good money maker. I guess I'd say yeah, he is. But I don't know if—"

"I'm sorry. Of course. I wasn't thinking. He's funding your business acquisition. I didn't mean to try to poach your investor. I didn't realize before—"

"No," I said. "He's not a business partner. That wouldn't be prudent, would it? Going into business with my boyfriend."

Again, as though he realized I might be able to help, he turned on the charm. "Well, I can see you are a sharp businesswoman. Maybe I should be pitching my opportunity to you. If you weren't already otherwise engaged, that is."

Crap. My set up had backfired. He was right. Who could be buying a taxidermy shop, while working there, and also be able to invest with him? It wouldn't hold water.

"So what do you say? Would you be willing to put in a word for me with Mike?"

"I don't know." *Damn.* I needed to get control of this thing. I could tell him I had cash, an inheritance, something, and keep Mike out of it. But my gut told me that'd be pushing it too far.

"You're right," he said, pulling away. He glanced back up at the mounted eagle, perched on a branch, a dead fish in its talons and mumbled, "If only they wanted 'em like that."

For better or worse, for now, I was stuck with his infatuation with Mike as an investor. "Well, what would I say? Please talk with Hal because I asked?"

Hal frowned. He had the possibility right in front of him. But he had to get through me.

At least he was still trying.

"You gotta give me a good reason," I said, "something he'd actually be interested in. What is it you're looking for exactly? How much are we talking?"

He blew out some air, resigned to giving up some details. "I've got this gig going, a sales train, all set up. I'm having trouble filling orders."

"You've got a supply and demand problem?"

"Yeah. You get it. A supply and demand problem." He fidgeted. "Actually, more of an inventory problem."

"I don't follow."

"Oh, I've got demand. I'm stuck on the supply chain." He turned to face me. "But I can tell you, there's a lot of money to be made."

"Well, if that's true, I'm sure he'd be interested," I said with some sarcasm, implying Mike was all about the money. "What are you selling?"

His eyes narrowed. "You know, I really appreciate this, but I'd prefer to talk the details with him." He smiled. "Thanks for bringing me in here. It's a real treat. And I hope you'll put in a word for me with Mike."

"I'll see what I can do, but I can't make any promises."

He gestured toward the cheetah. "That story seemed too good to be true. But there it is. That's something, to take down a cat like that. Man, that'd be something."

Oh, it really is something, to take down a predator. Wait till I take you *down.*

CHAPTER 12

"What is that smell?" I asked Jim.

"It's the glue I use. Sorry."

He was working on a bobcat.

Why would anyone want to kill a bobcat? I shook my head. I would never understand.

The shop had been quiet all morning and I got caught up on some paperwork, but I couldn't stop thinking about Hal and how I was going to approach Mike with the idea.

Oh, darn it, McVie, just call him. I punched in the numbers on my cell phone.

"Mike?"

"Yeah, Poppy. What's up?"

"I, uh, was thinking that we never really got a chance to get to know each other like we'd planned, you know, work on our cover, I mean, I'm fine with winging it, but I thought maybe we could—"

"Oh, yeah, sorry about that. I got sidetracked by a thing. You're right. We need to do that. For sure."

"Will you be at the house tonight? I could bring some takeout on the way. Maybe we could chat over dinner?"

"That sounds great. But I tell you what, I'll take care of dinner."

"Um. Okay." My stomach clenched.

"Don't worry. I remember. No meat."

I relaxed. He'd read my mind. "Right. Thanks. See you then."

At six o'clock, I closed the shop and headed to the mansion.

As I opened the door, the scent of sautéed onions filled my nostrils. I hung my coat in the closet and made my way to the kitchen.

Mike was at the cooktop, stirring something in a big pot, a chef's apron tied at his waist. "Good evening," he said with a bright smile.

"Good evening to you."

He set down the spoon, wiped his hands on the apron, and took two wine glasses from the cupboard. "I understand you are quite the wine connoisseur. I took the liberty of choosing a pinot noir. I hope it's to your liking." He'd already decanted the bottle. "The man down at the wine shop said this one had won several awards." He poured the two glasses to the correct amount, about one third full, handed me mine, and held his up. "Here's to new partners."

"To new partners," I said and clinked his glass.

I took a sip. Nice. A bit of spice. Light finish.

"Well," he asked, waiting. "What do you think?"

"It's delicious."

"I'm glad you like it."

The pot bubbled over. He set down his glass and quickly moved the pot off the flame. "You've distracted me," he said with a wink.

There it was. I was a distraction. What was it with men?

"Is there anything I can do to help?" I glanced at the small table that was tucked into a nook in the corner of the kitchen, a built-in bench seat on one side, one chair on the other. It was already set with salads and silverware for two.

"Nope. All set," he said. "I thought we'd eat in here. Much more cozy than the big formal dining room."

Cozy? "Yes," I said, suddenly feeling like this was a date. But there was no one we had to keep up the act for. "You didn't have to go to all this trouble. Honestly, take out would have been fine."

"Oh, c'mon," he said. "I don't get much opportunity to show off my amazing cooking skills. You don't grow up in an Italian family and order take out."

I took another sip of the wine. *Okay then.* Was he flirting with me? *Oh no.* What if he was? I had to step carefully. *Oh stop. Of course he's not. He's just being friendly.*

He moved about the kitchen with confidence. A boiling pot of water and pasta was poured into a colander in the sink. Spaghetti. That was plated, a red sauce spooned over it, cheese sprinkled on the top. Then warm bread was pulled from the oven. All choreographed like a ballet.

"Take a seat," he said, carrying the plates to the table.

I slid into the booth seat. He set down the plates, went back for the bread, then removed his apron and took the chair.

"So. Shall we?"

I leaned forward, took in the savory scents of the sauce—oregano, basil, garlic. "You've outdone yourself."

"My grandma's recipe. She's from the old country."

I raised my glass. "*Salute. Cento di questi giorni.*"

"Ah," he said, grinning wide. "*Tu parli italiano.*"

"I speak several languages," I said.

"Impressive." His smile was genuine.

"Not really. I was a Navy brat. Lived all over the world."

"Well, still," he said.

"And you, where are you from?" I asked, setting down the glass. I twirled spaghetti around my spoon.

"New Jersey. I played basketball in high school. Dreamed of being a police detective. Somewhere along the way, I decided to apply for the F.B.I. and ended up in drug enforcement. Never married. When would I find the time?"

"Wow, that is a brief summary."

"Well, I'd rather hear about you."

Charming. "You didn't mention how you acquired your

acting skills."

"Oh that. That comes from a childhood on the streets. You learn to deal with whatever is thrown at you. I bet you got your share of training the same way."

He asked all about me, about what it was like growing up as a military kid. He wanted to know about my passion for animals. He couldn't get enough of the story of how I'd caught Ray Goldman, the whale hunter, and, all the while he had me talking, I couldn't figure out how to broach the subject of meeting with Hal.

"And a husband? Boyfriend?" he asked.

"Nope."

He smiled. "I thought maybe you and Dalton."

"Oh, gosh no. I mean, he's a great partner. But we're like oil and water."

"Yeah, he seems like a by-the-book kinda guy."

I nodded. Did that mean he wasn't?

"I admire that. In some ways."

"What do mean?"

"Well, I'm not ashamed to admit, sometimes I want justice to be swift. I get frustrated by the line of the law, you know. Animals aren't afforded enough protection. You know what I mean?"

"Yeah." I nodded, grinning inside. Maybe this would be easier than I'd thought. "If only the penalties were commensurate with the real crime to them."

"Yeah. Commensurate." He held up his glass. "Damn right. Murder is murder."

I clinked his glass with mine, nodding in agreement as I took another sip.

"Mike, I wanted to ask if you—"

"Oh, I almost forgot." He rose from the chair, set his napkin on the table. "Dessert is in the oven."

"Oh, my. Dessert? But I'm already stuffed. The pasta was delicious."

"Well, we've got all night," he said as he pulled something heavenly from the oven. "Chocolate amaretti cake. My mom's favorite recipe. I thought you might like it."

"You had me at chocolate."

He set it on a wire rack to cool, slipped off the oven mitts, and returned to the table.

Sitting across from me, he stared for a long moment before he said, "You know what, Poppy? You're not at all what I imagined."

"Yeah, what was that?"

"Oh, I don't know. Obnoxious. Spoiled. Annoying."

I laughed. So, Dalton had been telling the truth.

He took another drink of the wine, his eyes on me.

I felt a little flush come to my cheeks.

"I admit," he said. "Honestly, I thought you'd be a princess. But I think you and I are cut from the same cloth."

"I'm glad you think so."

He leaned forward. "What happens out there sometimes, what doesn't get seen, doesn't need to be reported." A tiny grin formed at the corner of his mouth. "As long as the job gets done. Right?"

I nodded. I'd been worried I'd have to finesse my way in, to slyly convince him to meet with Hal. What a relief. A conversation with Dalton would have been one long fight. Now, I felt confident Mike might be willing to give it a try.

"Are you saying you've crossed the line before?" I asked, containing my excitement.

"Would you turn me in?" he asked, teasing.

"When I think about what the criminals get away with? No way. Besides, if I knew, I'd probably be right beside you."

"Good to know."

He refilled our glasses and placed a divine slice of chocolate heaven in front of me.

I slipped a forkful into my mouth. "Oh. My. God," I said, letting my eyelashes flutter as I held the yummy cake in my

110 · Kimberli A. Bindschatel

mouth, savoring it for a long moment before swallowing.

"Hit the spot, huh?"

I set down my fork. "I have something to ask you."

"You sound serious."

"I am. It's a favor, really."

"You want me to finish your dessert for you?"

I grinned. "No. Not on your life."

We both smiled. It was nice.

"The favor. It's a long shot."

"I like long shots."

"Risky."

"I like risky."

"And maybe not so…by-the-book."

"Now, I'm really intrigued."

I drew in a breath. To explain to Mike, I had to admit I'd crossed the line, that I'd sent Chris, a civilian, undercover for me. I'd have to trust him. I hesitated.

"Look, people in glass houses, you know. I admit, I've bent a few rules along the way. You can trust me."

He was my partner. On my team. *Here goes.* "Okay. You know the guy, Hal, the one I asked you to invite to the party?"

"Yeah, the fidgety one?"

"Yeah. Well, he comes into the shop all the time. Jim knew his first name. But we had nothing on the books about him. He never buys. Just stops in, looks around, asks weird questions. I watched the videos of him. Odd behavior. Wasn't making any sense."

"Yeah?"

"So, when he came in the shop one day, I followed him." I waited. Would he scold me for it?

"And?"

"And, he plans parties for wealthy kids. You know, these elaborate shindigs for the ultra rich."

Mike sat back in the chair, laced his hands together. "Ah, the owl salesman. Why didn't you tell me?"

"I needed to be sure."

"And now you're sure?"

"Well." I looked him in the eyes. "Hyland said to drop it."

He waved his hand as if to ignore her. "She's got her head in the clouds. And talk about by-the-book." He shook his head. "She's never spent a day in the field. She has no idea how it works, how you gotta connect the dots on the fly. How sometimes it's all about trusting your gut."

I smiled. "Exactly."

He leaned forward. "So, what'd you find?"

"I don't have any more proof, if that's what you mean. No actual confirmation of live owls. But I talked to him, at the party. He was cagey, but he didn't deny anything either. The thing is, he shifted the conversation to wanting an investor. For something. He seemed fixated on you, being a super rich guy and, well, morally aligned with his way of business."

"You think he wants to ask me to invest in the owl trafficking scheme?"

"Yes, that's what I think." I bit my lip. "I know it's a distraction. I know Hyland already told me not to pursue it. I know it's a long shot. And I know we're coming down to the line on this operation and—"

"The clock is ticking, yes."

"But my gut tells me it's real. It's not a bait and switch. He's really selling owls. If you would just talk to him, see what he says."

Mike grinned at me. "Well, what are we waiting for?"

CHAPTER 13

So far so good. Part one, done—convincing Mike to take the risk. Next was going to be the big test. If Mike could convince Hal to trust him, we'd have a case. I could do this. Trust my teammate. And he was good. Really good.

Hal wouldn't come out to the mansion. Not sure why. He wanted Mike to meet him downtown at some ritzy cigar bar. It was apparent that he didn't want me there either. Too bad. This was my bust and I was in all the way. Besides, Mike bringing me along showed Hal who was calling the shots. Hal needed to think he had to impress Mike, not the other way around.

Mike and I arrived in the sports car. I hadn't returned the fur coat, so I wore that, too. Hal was holed up in a booth in the back, like some gangster, a couple of expensive cigars already on his table.

As the maître d' seated us, Hal ordered a bourbon on the rocks for Mike.

"Another Jim Beam, sir?" the maître d' asked.

"No, no." Hal shook his head, squirming. "What would you like, Mike? Pappy Van Winkle interest you?

"Ah, you know bourbon," Mike said, acting impressed.

"I do my homework."

"A Pappy Van Winkle would be wonderful."

Hal nodded at the maître d', and shooed him away without a mention of me. The real Poppy would have given him a tongue lashing about old school misogyny, but this fur-coat-wearing Poppy let it slide.

Hal launched into his spiel. "Well, first of all, thanks for coming. I know you're going to—"

Mike held up his hand to silence him. "Well, *first of all*, my lady would like a drink."

Slap. I did love how this man played a character.

"Oh, oh, sorry." Hal was on his feet, waving for the bartender.

To me, Mike said, "Would you like to see the wine list, babe?"

"And a glass of the house red," Hal shouted, way too loudly.

I rolled my eyes. Mike winked at me.

Hal settled back in his seat.

"Sorry. Sorry about that. I'm just so excited you're here. I've got a great opportunity for you."

"Well, let's hear it," Mike said, impatient, glancing at his watch. "Whatcha got?"

"Right."

Hal had, no doubt, an idea in his head about how this was going to play out. Mike was purposefully flustering him. He stared at him, intimidating as could be. Funny how Hal had been so confident when talking to me. But in the presence of power and money, he'd turned into a nervous Nellie.

"Right." Hal screwed up his face. He looked around the cigar bar, his eyes all jittery, then brought his attention back to Mike. "Okay, okay. I have this gig going. Rich parents. More money than they know what to do with. Spoiled kids." He leaned in closer. "They'll pay anything."

Mike stared at him, blank-faced, unimpressed. "And?"

"And, what does a ten year old want more than anything?"

Mike stared at him, deadpan. "I have no idea."

"I sell them pet owls, man. It's practically like printing money."

"Owls?" Mike said as if Hal had offered him a three-eyed space alien.

"I got parents coming in everyday wanting the biggest, best, most unique present for their special spawn. It's unbelievable really. All I've got to do is hint at it and they start salivating."

"But pet owls? Do owls even make good pets?"

"No. I don't know." He squirmed in the seat. "I mean, who cares. It's what the kids want. They're obsessed with Harry Potter. That's the point."

"Harry Potter?"

"Dude. You don't know who Harry Potter is? The kid's stories. You know, wizards and magic."

"I know who Harry Potter is. What does he have to do with owls?"

"The wizard kids, in the stories, they have these magical pet owls, dude."

Mike sat back, twisted his ring around his finger, eyeing Hal up and down. "Selling an owl is illegal."

Hal's face turned a whiter shade of pale. He pursed his lips. His eyes flitted over to me, then back to Mike. His tongue shot out of his mouth, licked his bottom lip. Then, as if he'd gathered some gumption, his eyes narrowed and he leaned forward. "Dude, so is shooting an eagle. I didn't think you'd give a shit about owls, man."

Mike slowly turned to me. "You took him up to my room?"

I gave him a pouty lip. "I'm just so proud of you, baby."

He turned back to Hal. "I don't give a shit about owls. But what you're talking about is an illegal enterprise." Mike put great emphasis on the word enterprise.

Hal fidgeted some more. Then finally nodded acknowledgment. "Yeah."

Mike twisted the ring again. "How much money are we talking?"

Hal seemed to relax. "I got 'em paying five large."

"Five grand?" Mike said, incredulous. "For one bird?"

Hal's head bobbed with excitement.

"Do you even tell them it's illegal?"

He swallowed. His Adam's apple looked like it got stuck in his throat. He squeaked out. "Yeah. They don't care, man. Like I said, anything for little Johnny."

"But still. Owls? For pets?"

"They're easy. You get a big bird cage and feed 'em, I don't know, bird seed or something. Whatever. Who cares? What matters is, the brats want 'em."

He didn't even know what they eat?

"I see what you're saying," Mike said. He was giving Hal a morsel. "How do you get 'em?"

"I got that worked out."

Mike gave his glass of bourbon a turn. "Well, in that case, I don't see what you need me for."

Hal looked around the room again before answering. "I know I can expand. But I need to set up a little place to keep 'em. Here in Chicago. You know, I can't have 'em in my apartment. And these damn parents, it's like they don't remember their own kids' birthdays. They come in and want a party fit for a king and they want it next week. Shit, I can't get a bird here that fast. I mean, like I said, getting the birds ain't the problem. I got that all worked out. It's the time it takes to get 'em here. Right now, I can only offer one to the parents who plan a little more in advance. But I'm telling you, there's all this opportunity, you know. Money to be made."

Chris had told Hal his party was two months out. What a lucky break. Otherwise, Hal wouldn't have even made the offer.

"You're telling me," Mike said, "that you've got unlimited clients, each willing to shell out five grand for an illegal bird, and you've also got some source to get as many birds as you need, you've just got an inventory problem. This is a cash flow thing? That about sum it up?"

"Yeah, man. I just need—"

"You're full of shit." Mike downed the rest of the bourbon and rose from the chair. "C'mon honey, let's go."

What? I couldn't bring myself to get up from the chair. Mike was taking a bold chance. Cash flow was an easy problem to solve, with half a brain. What if Hal let us walk away?

Hal looked down at his hands, picked at his fingernails. I let my coat slide to the floor, stalling. As I started to rise, Hal burst out, "Dude, don't go man. I'm not yanking your chain. It's for real."

Mike hesitated.

"I'll show you my books. I got filthy rich parents coming out of my ears."

"Oh, I don't doubt that," Mike said. "It's the birds I got issue with. Harry Potter's owl is a snowy. They only live in the arctic. Way the hell on the edge of nowhere. How you catching them? How you transporting them? And most important, how the hell are you getting them into the country?"

"Dude, I told you I got that part worked out. I got a guy—" He hesitated, as though he didn't want to give away his whole operation. "He catches 'em, you know, keeps 'em alive. I call when I need one. But I got a full time job, right, the source for the clients. I can't be driving back and forth every time I sell one. That's the problem."

A guy? So Hal *has* set up a whole supply chain?

Mike shook his head. "Forget it." He grabbed me by the arm. "Get your coat."

"Don't go." He looked pained. "It's legit. I can prove it."

Mike looked at me, thinking. He wasn't giving Hal the slightest break.

"I'm telling you I can prove it."

Mike eased back into the chair, crossed his arms, and eyed Hal. "You led me to believe this was a cash flow problem. That you had everything else worked out."

"I do."

"No. You're saying you have a source, some guy, works

for you, who already has the birds. They're already caught, in cages, I presume." He leaned forward. "But the only little snag is timing? So the border is the problem? No shit genius. Figuring out how to get live, illegal birds through customs is the key to the whole thing. If you don't have that, then—"

"No, no," Hal said, sitting up straight. "No. I'm telling you. It's all worked out. The border's not an issue."

Mike gave him a look of warning.

He shook his head, shifted in his seat. "I'm not lying. I got it all worked out except for a place to keep 'em alive here. Up there, my guy, he takes care of the birds. I pick one up, deliver it straight to the parents, no problem. But if I get, say, five at a time, so as I have some ready to sell, I gotta have some way to hold 'em here."

"Yeah, you already said all that. The problem is"—Mike shook his head, as though he didn't believe any of it—"I don't like it. That doesn't jive. Besides, even if it did, too many unknown variables. Live birds? Too many ways for money to go down the drain." Mike rubbed his chin. "Nope. I don't like it."

Smart. Mike wasn't making a big issue about the border part.

Hal leaned forward. "What percent you want? Fifty percent? What?"

"Fifty percent of what? So far, this has all been talk," Mike said, his expression exasperated. "This it too good to be true. I haven't even seen a bird. I tell you what, you want me to invest, I'm calling your bluff."

Hal's face fell.

Wow, Mike was good. He set the hook in Hal, acknowledging it was worth investing in, if it were true, and gave him incentive to give us what we want—proof.

"I could, I suppose, I could get a bird. If you give me a couple days."

Mike shrugged, pushed the empty bourbon glass to the center of the table. "So, you can get one bird. And show me some ledgers. That doesn't prove shit."

"I could…maybe," Hal burst, "make arrangements to take you there. If that's what it takes. Show you."

"Show me what?"

"Dude, show you the birds."

Was he serious? That was bold.

"*Dude,*" Mike said, mocking him. "Do you think I'm an idiot?"

"No." Hal sat back. He didn't know what Mike was getting at.

"I'm not going all the way to the arctic circle on some wild goose chase. You don't seem to get—"

"Arctic circle? No, man. It's just over the border." His gaze went to his fingernails again. "The birds. Where they're kept. It's just over the border."

Well, I'll be damned. No wonder customs wasn't an issue. He's walking them over. That's what was taking the time.

"You kidding me?"

"Nope." Hal shook his head, confident he was getting somewhere with Mike. "I can arrange it. Just give me a day or two."

"Yeah, whatever," Mike said, keeping to character. "I won't hold my breath."

Hal kept nodding. "I'll make it work. You'll see. Then we'll talk investment."

Mike already had me by the arm, walking me out.

"I knew it!" I said, back in the car. "I knew he was really selling owls. Bait and switch, she said. No way. This is for real, Mike."

He nodded, grinning. He was excited, too.

"That was impressive," I said. "The way you walked him right where you wanted him to go."

"Yeah, well, we'll see if he actually comes through."

"What do you think he meant, though, about the time it took to get the birds? That wasn't clear."

"I think he means an actual logistical problem."

"That's what I was thinking."

"Maybe he gets them across the border by bicycle, who knows? We'll find out."

"Yeah," I said with a grin. *But...* "Seems odd, doesn't it? That he set this whole supply chain up but didn't plan for inventory here in Chicago."

"Not really. He's a typical idiot who stumbled onto a good thing."

"I don't know. I'm just saying, he went to a lot of trouble to set up the supply chain though. He had to be pretty clever, and to not think that part through—"

"Like I said, he probably had no idea he'd be able to sell so many and ran out of cash to invest. That's why he came looking for me."

"I suppose." Something wasn't right. "So we take this to Hyland now?"

"No. Not yet. You know how she reacted last time. He could still be yanking our chain. Let's wait to see what he does now."

I nodded. That seemed reasonable.

"Good job, McVie." He gave me a wink.

At 7:35 a.m., I was on the train, on my way to the shop, when my phone buzzed. The boss was calling an unexpected, mandatory meeting today at noon.

I texted Dalton. He'd gotten the same message. No idea what was up.

By the time noon came, I'd paced a hole in the carpet. What could it be about?

Back I went to the same drab downtown building, the same office with the fluorescent light. Tom, Mike, Dalton and I sat around the same table, waiting.

Finally, at 12:15 p.m., the door swung open and in she came. She took her chair at the head of the table and looked at Mike.

"Well, fill me in."

"Some significant new information has come to light on a suspect, one Hal Gruba."

What? I stared. Significant new information? We'd agreed we wouldn't bring him up to Ms. Hyland until we had more concrete proof. Had Mike learned something new since last night? Why didn't he tell me?

"He's a regular down at Wilson's shop. We don't have much intel on him because he never buys anything. He comes in, asks Jim some seemingly benign questions, and then leaves again. His behavior has never made sense, so I've been keeping a close eye on him."

Wait. What?

Dalton looked at me, eyebrows raised.

"And?" Ms. Hyland said.

"I had suspicions about him before we arrested Jim. But like I said, we couldn't pin him down with anything. For months, I've been watching, waiting."

No way. You didn't know who he was until I pointed him out at the banquet.

"Somewhere along the way, I learned he was a party planner, so when Poppy here mentioned some party planner had made the offer to sell an owl, well, I got to wondering if that guy and Hal were one and the same. Turns out, bingo."

Okay. Maybe he was trying to cover for me, make an explanation for the connection.

"When I saw his name on the list of attendees at the banquet—"

When you saw his name? I saw his name.

"I invited him to the private party, to see if I couldn't get him talking. Turns out he's been looking for an investor for his trafficking operation. Well, with my cover as a rich guy, I worked it. Then last night, at a meet I set up, he revealed to me that indeed, he is bringing owls across the border. He's made the offer to show me the operation."

"Great work connecting the dots, Wessell," Ms. Hyland said, visibly impressed.

My pulse rate went for the stratosphere.

"I'd like to pursue this," Mike went on. "As soon as he comes back with an actual meet up, I'd like to know I have a green light."

"You do." She nodded, considering something. "One conversation, though, and he's offered to show you the operation?"

Actually, I've had several conversations with him. I've been working him for days.

Mike nodded. "Money talks."

"Maybe. But that's still too easy. Make sure to keep backup protocol with Special Agent McVie."

Yes!

"That's not going to work," Mike said. "He's shown concern about anyone else and it'd be awkward, bringing the girlfriend along. I can handle it."

My mouth dropped open. *What? But I'm the one who brought him to you.* "Actually," I said, "I have been building a relationship, both at the shop, and—"

Hyland shook her head. "Take Special Agent Dalton then. Create a scenario to make it work."

"Yes, ma'am," Mike said with an affirmative nod.

Hyland rose to leave and we were all out of our chairs. Just like that.

Steam came out of my ears. Not only had Mike hijacked my case, he'd successfully pushed me out.

CHAPTER 14

"That son-of-a-bitch!"

"Poppy, take a deep breath." Dalton sat on the edge of the bed, taking his boots off. He'd taken me to his hotel room so we could talk in private.

"Where does he get off? That was my perp, my discovery! And he stole it from me. Right from under me. Pushed me right out. Without a second thought."

"Are you sure that's what happened? Maybe you misunderstood him. I mean, did he think you were bringing Hal to him? If so, he would—"

"Misunderstood? Misunderstood! No, he understood all too well. He understood the scope of what I'd discovered from the beginning. That's probably what he's been doing these last weeks, when he was supposed to be getting into character with me, when he came in so late, left so early. He was investigating Hal, confirming my claim. He planned to take this over from the get go."

"You don't know that."

"That snake!"

"Start from the beginning. What did you tell him? How did he learn about Hal?"

"I can't believe this!"

Dalton rose from the bed, put his hands on my shoulders, made me look into his eyes. "I know you're angry."

"Angry? I've livid. I'm outraged. I'm pissed!"

"Okay, I didn't have the right word." He was talking with that calm voice. "But I'm with you. That was a crappy way to handle it. It seemed like he took all the credit, but—"

"Seemed like? He didn't even mention me. He made it look like I was too clueless to put the pieces of the puzzle together and, of course, he did."

"I wouldn't say—"

"Some kind of partner. Some kind of team. This is crap. That's what this is. Bullshit."

"You're right. He was an ass. Whether he misunderstood roles or purposefully took all the credit. Whatever. You're right. But at least you got what you wanted. Hyland approved going after Hal."

"Yeah." I crossed my arms. "Without me."

"I know that makes you angry."

I frowned.

"Okay, pissed. But sometimes that's how it works. Why is this so important to you? What do you have to prove, anyway?"

My teeth clenched together so hard I thought my jawbone might crack. "Bullshit. That's what this is."

"Yes. That is, actually, a very common synonym for teamwork. But then, there are those times when you know your team's got your back."

"Yeah, like at the paintball training? He talked me into running in for that flag. I knew we shouldn't rush, but he pushed me. He did it on purpose. He used me as a sacrificial lamb, to find out where you were hiding."

Dalton nodded. "You're probably right."

"You call that teamwork?"

"Nope."

"He's a self-centered, arrogant, lying son-of-a-bitch."

"Yep. And now we know that about him."

I crossed my arms again, frowned.

"Just more information, that's all," Dalton said.

"Yeah, but still. He's... He's a... It's not right."

He stood before me, moved into my line of vision, forcing me to look at him. "Do you want me to kick his ass for you? Because I will."

I grinned, relaxed a little. "Oh Dalton. What was I thinking?" I plopped down on the edge of the bed. "I feel so stupid. How could I be so naïve?"

"Why? For believing what he told you? For seeing the good in people?"

"Yeah, well...lot of good it does. It's just so...humiliating. I mean, we're supposed to be a team. He was supposed to be my partner. And he just, he just...tossed me aside like I was... some useless hassle that'd just be in his way. What the hell? I'm the one who brought Hal to him. I handed him over on a silver platter." I looked up at Dalton. "I thought I could trust him."

"Oh Poppy." He took my hand, pulled me to my feet, and wrapped his arms around me. "You did nothing wrong. You should have been able to trust him."

I leaned into his shoulder and drew in a breath. "I'm such a fool."

"No, you're not. You're a brilliant woman with excellent instincts." He pulled back, looked into my eyes. "This is all about his ego. It has nothing to do with you or your skills as an agent."

"Yeah, well..."

"Yeah, well, nothing. He hasn't seen you in action yet. He has no idea what an asset you are. If he had, you'd be his first choice to be by his side. No doubt about it."

I sighed. Dalton was trying so hard to make me feel better.

"I hate to admit it, but this really is a good thing though, for me," he said with a grin.

"What? Why?"

"He probably hasn't noticed yet that you're so damn gorgeous."

That made me blush. I turned away. I had to get myself

together.

I looked around Dalton's hotel room. "Seems funny, being in your hotel room. I'd kinda thought if I ever ended up here, it would be because—" I caught myself.

His expression changed to a hopeful smile. "It would be because?"

"Because you wanted me here."

"I do want you here."

"Well, I mean…"

One eyebrow went up. "Like, maybe, for some time alone together." His eyes held mine.

"I thought you were worried about distractions."

"I was. I am. I mean, c'mon." He eased toward me, put his hands on my hips, tugged me toward him. "You know this is complicated."

I melted a little.

"We can't ever show our true feelings. To anyone. Not on the job. Not undercover."

"And what are our true feelings?"

His gaze turned soft. His hands came up under my chin as he leaned forward and kissed me. All the rage I'd been holding in turned into a different kind of heat and burned through me. Next thing I knew, we were on the bed, my legs tangled in his, his hands tangled in my hair. His kisses behind my ear.

He rolled me over onto my back, kissed down my neck, pushing my collar away.

I wanted this. I needed this.

His hand slid under my shirt, up my back, and my shirt was off. I tugged at his, pulling it over his head. I wrapped my arms around his back and pulled him toward me as I pressed up against him. I couldn't get close enough.

His hot breath on my neck made me quiver.

Being here, with him, felt so natural, so right, yet as though it set loose a need I didn't know I'd had. I'd longed for this moment, hoped he'd wanted it, too.

I pulled back to look into his eyes for a sweet moment. God, he was so damn handsome. Then I kissed him. His kiss was like the rest of him: on fire. His tongue caressed mine as my fingers tugged at his hair.

His phone rang. He started to pull away, but I grabbed hold of him. "Let it go," I whispered.

"But I can't—"

I pressed my lips to his, pushed my tongue inside, wanting more.

Ring, ring.

"Poppy, I have to—"

I opened my eyes and the ceiling came into focus. "Dammit!"

"I'm sorry. I was told to standby. I have to get it." He rolled onto his side, dug the phone from his pocket, clicked to answer as he sat upright, and held the phone to his ear. "Uh huh. Yep. Gotcha. Uh huh. I'll be there." He ended the call.

He turned to me and frowned.

"What?" I asked.

"It was Mike. It's a go. Sometime tonight."

I sat up. "Just like that? He convinced Hal to let you go?"

He shrugged. "It seems so."

All the rage was back. "That rat bastard." I got to my feet. "Mike Wessell. I'm going to call him Mike weasel from now on. Weasel. That's what he is. A weasel."

Dalton flopped on the bed, let out a sigh.

"And that's not even fair to weasels. He's a liar. He flat out, stone-faced lied."

He sat back up. "Uh huh."

"I mean, who does that? Does he have no conscience? How does he justify it in his mind? Does he believe the lies coming out of his own mouth?"

"I don't know," Dalton mumbled. "You're not going to let this go, are you?"

"Let this go? What, smile and nod and go along with it?"

"Yeah, that's the definition of letting something go."

"Are you kidding?"

He slouched. "Unfortunately, no, I was not."

"And what's it to you? *You* get to go with him. You." I grabbed my shirt and tugged it back on. "Why'd it have to be you? I'm the one who figured it out. What'd you do? Nothing. You told me to forget about Hal."

Dalton stared at me, too smart to reply.

I turned away from him and went to the window. Dalton's room was on the twelfth floor. There was no view of Lake Michigan from here. Just more tall buildings.

I felt caged, captive in this city. I couldn't breathe. I needed the forest. I needed trees. Space. Fresh air.

"So what are you going to do about it?" Dalton said to my backside.

Bang! A bird smacked into the window. I jumped back. "What in the world!"

Dalton was beside me. "Yeah, I heard one yesterday. It's the reflection on the windows."

"Well, I know that but—why don't architects get it? We've known for years and years that slanted windows saves birds' lives. It's so frustrating."

Dalton nodded.

"It's our own stupidity. We could save more birds if only—" *That's it.* Hal. He'd said something about dead birds. They'd be easier. Or something like that. Why didn't I realize it then? That had to be one of the reasons he kept hanging around at the taxidermy shop. He was losing a lot of the owls. During transport? While caged? All raptors, but owls in particular, were very sensitive to captivity. It made sense that, without trained care specialists, a lot of the birds would die.

The answer had been right in front of me and I missed it. He was looking for an investor but also, no doubt, thinking of a secondary market. Maybe he could sell the dead owls, stuffed for display, if he could find a taxidermist willing to do the illegal work.

"What are you thinking about?" Dalton asked.

Selling stuffed owls was one thing, but they couldn't possibly be worth as much as live owls. If he could decrease the mortality rate, he'd make a lot more money. I needed to convince him I knew exactly how to do that.

"I don't like that look on your face," Dalton said. "I've seen that look. What's going on in that brain of yours?"

"Nothing," I said. "You're right. I need to let this go. And I need to get back to work." I gave him a peck on the lips and was out the door.

CHAPTER 15

Before I got to the elevator, I had my phone to my ear. "Chris? Listen. I need you to call Hal back. Make an appointment. For this afternoon. Tell him you're only in town for one day and you have to see him. Whatever. Make it happen."

"But I'm not in town. I'm in Mumbai."

"Doesn't matter. I'm going to meet with him. I just need you to make the appointment to be sure he's going to be there. Okay? Call him right now and let me know when."

"Are you sure that's a good idea?"

"No, but do it anyway." I paused. "Please."

"Oh, all right."

Five minutes later he called me back with confirmation. The meeting was scheduled for four o'clock. I had three hours.

"Okay. At five minutes to four, call and cancel. I don't want him to connect us."

"Fine. But for the record, I don't think you should do this."

"Noted."

Within an hour, I had Mr. Anderson, the Audubon Chapter President, on the phone. He referred me to an avian care specialist who he felt would be helpful.

Hannah, a nice young woman with a cheerful voice, was more than willing to fill me in on caring for owls. Her passion was contagious. "They're highly susceptible to stress," she said. "No doubt, in the situation you describe, there'd be a high mortality rate, as you say."

"Yes, well, I need to convince them, in a very short time, that I know how to fix that. Can you give me a primer?"

"Well, are they capturing adult birds or stealing owlets from the nests?"

"I don't know. Does it make a difference?"

"If they get owlets young enough, they could imprint on the handler and be easier to manage. But raising an owl from a chick takes a long time and a lot of care. Not to mention, snowy owls can be very aggressive when they defend their nests. It would be hard to steal the owlets."

She was thinking like a conservationist, not a criminal. I didn't have the heart to tell her that no owl poacher was going to fight with the adult owl. They'd just shoot it and walk up and take the babies.

"But the thing is, these birds breed in very remote areas in the arctic circle," she went on. "Just getting there would be extreme."

I'd thought of that, but said nothing, letting her continue her train of thought.

"If I had to guess, I'd say they are capturing adult owls in their winter feeding grounds. They are probably baiting them in areas where they are most likely to visit."

"And that would be southern Canada, say Ontario, or Quebec?"

"Those are where the highest concentration of snowy owls would be in winter, yes."

"And they would use nets, or something like that?"

"There are lots of ways to catch an owl. None are good for the owl, if you aren't careful. They can panic, break a wing. I hate to think about it."

"Okay, well, how about if you guess, for me, as to what is the most likely cause of the high mortality rate."

"Like I said, owls can easily get stressed and stress can kill them. They aren't meant to be in a cage. When we have injured birds here, we make sure their enclosures are covered, to avoid too much visual stimuli, and we try to make sure the area around them is really quiet. And especially for snowies, it needs to be cool. They're intolerant of heat."

"That's good to know. How do you recognize when they are stressed?"

"Well, let me see. I just know." She giggled. "How do I know? Well, sometimes, not always, they'll pluck their own feathers out. Oh, and they'll exhibit gular fluttering. That's where they open their beaks really wide and the throat pulses, in and out, sort of like they're panting. I've even seen owls that look drunk. They blink with one eye, then the other. The worst is when they panel breathe. You can see the chest moving, like they're huffing, and the tail is bobbing. That's a really bad sign. Not good."

"Anything else I should know?"

"Not that I can think of. Good luck."

"Thanks."

I ran down the list of notes I'd made. Not much to go on. I'd have to stick to basics.

Right at four o'clock, I walked into Hal's office.

I had one shot at this. It had to work.

When he saw me, his eyes grew wide. He rushed to the door, looked outside, both ways, then slammed it shut behind me. "What are you doing here? You can't come here."

"Why not?"

"Well, because. What if someone sees you? And connects us? What if we're seen?"

"What if we are?"

"Well, I can't take that risk."

"Relax. I don't have 'criminal' stamped on my forehead. I

could very well be here inquiring about a birthday party for my brat kid."

"Yeah, well." He crossed his arms. "What are you really doing here? Mike and I have already made our plans to—"

"Yeah, I know." I sat down in the chair, made myself comfortable. "Mike's a brilliant man, really,"—*and a rotten snake*—"when it comes to investments, building a business, no one better. You should definitely partner with him."

"Okay?" He crossed his arms. "So, why are you here?"

Here goes. "Well, I've been thinking about our conversation and you mentioned a problem that I think I can help you with."

His fingers tapped on his elbows. "Yeah?"

"I've got—"

"Wait." He rolled his eyes. "Mike said you'd want in on the business. He told me I shouldn't talk about the details with you."

Make that lower than a snake. "What? No. I don't want in on your pet owl business. I'm talking about a whole different thing."

His gummy lips pursed, that tongue came out of his mouth, licked at his bottom lip. "Is this some kind of bait and switch routine? What are you up to? You trying to pull some kind of good cop, bad cop thing on me?"

Ah, the irony of that.

He snugged his crossed arms tighter to his chest. "I'm not interested."

I couldn't lose him now. *Make it about the money.* "You're not interested in significantly increasing your profit? With a completely different revenue source? One Mike hasn't thought of. Because I can help you."

A flicker of curiosity crossed his face.

"The way I see it, you've got much more profit potential than you realize." Now I had him thinking. A little buttering up couldn't hurt. "Don't get me wrong. You've put together a brilliant business opportunity here. Impressive, by the way. Mike was playing the hardass, but he wants in. He told me."

That got a grin.

"The thing is, you two are focused on inventory. When in reality, you've got a much bigger issue with the cost of goods sold."

Hal relaxed a little. "Keep talking."

Whew. Now play it cool. "I'd be willing to bet, you have a lot of birds dying on you, right?"

He made a little nod.

"What's the mortality rate of the owls in your care?"

"Well…" He seemed more reluctant to share than that he didn't know the number. "Some."

Fine. "Even one seems like a lot of money being lost. At five grand a pop, retail, that seems like a place you'd want to improve your numbers. There's a cost of acquiring the birds, transporting them, caring for them until they're sold."

"Yeah?"

"Well, if four out of five birds die, that means you have five times the cost for one live bird. I'm thinking that there must be a secondary market for those birds. If they were mounted, of course." I paused. He said nothing. "Isn't that the reason you keep coming by the shop?"

"What are you saying?" He leaned back, curious now. "Are you wanting the work?"

I nodded, gave him a grin. "I think you and I could work out a deal."

He smiled.

Now, go in for the kill. "But the more I think about it, I wonder, if you could keep all the birds alive, you'd have more to sell at a lower cost of acquisition. That would mean a much higher profit. Much higher than selling stuffed birds."

He eyed me. Sat down in the chair. Looked me over some more.

"You know, I know a lot about living birds, too. How to care for them. What they eat. How to keep them safe and alive in transport."

He looked at me through squinted eyes.

"I bet with a few small changes, I can more than double your yield. Guaranteed."

"Double?" He didn't believe me. "And what do you want out of it?"

Crap. That was a good question. "It's a good will thing, you know, in doing business together. I help you, you help me." *Lame! Not a good reason. McVie! Think!* "I help you keep more alive, but any that still don't make it, you hire me to stuff 'em." *Okay, that might work.* "You make more money. Mike makes more money. I make more money. What do you say?"

He stared. Didn't say no. Was I getting somewhere with him?

I kept on. "Were not talking about a big commitment here. It's a tiny favor I'd be doing for you. Let me see your guy's care protocol. Show me how they're being fed, housed, and I'll give some tips. That's it. Easy peasy. I'm sure, with a few changes, you could keep a lot more of them alive and healthy to sell."

"But you need to see the birds to figure that out?"

"Well, yeah," I said, as though it were no big deal.

"And you can explain it all to him when we're there? What changes to make?"

"Sure can," I said, trying not to get too excited.

I was back in the game.

"Hold on," he said and pulled a phone from his pocket. He punched in some numbers, then held it to his ear as he paced. Someone must have answered because he said, "Hey, I've been trying all day to getcha." There was a long pause. "Yeah, sorry, sorry. I just—" his eyes connected with mine and he lowered his voice. "So you got my message?" Another pause. "Well, I got something else to talk to you about. Remember how we talked about so many birds dying? Well, I got someone who can—" Another pause. Hal nodded his head. "Yeah. Yeah," he said. "Yeah, tomorrow." He frowned. "Right. Just two. Okay."

He hung up.

He dialed another number. This person picked up right away. "Hey, Mike. I got confirmation to go tonight. Be at the train station in forty-five minutes?"

As he ended the call, he looked at me. "If you're going, I'm leaving right now."

I was born ready. "I'm ready," I said and was out of my chair.

"Oh wait," he said, thinking. "That's not gonna work."

"What? Why not?" My stomach sank.

"I have an errand to run. Why don't you meet me with Mike at the train station."

That wouldn't work. I couldn't alert Mike. I had to show up with Hal. "Are you sure? I don't mind a detour while you run an errand. Really. I'm ready to go right now."

He thought about it, sighed. "Well, I guess it would be okay."

Whew.

He grabbed his coat and I followed him out the door and around into the alley to a beat up old Chevy something. Blue. Four door. I got in the passenger seat.

"It will just take a minute on the way," he muttered.

The car grumbled to life and Hal sped down the Chicago streets.

After a stop at a fast food chicken shack, he pulled down a side street alley and parked behind a small, fifties-era three-flat. Red brick. No yard. A tiny one-car garage.

"Wait here," he said and fled from the car, the chicken dinner in his hands.

He wasn't gone five minutes and he was back.

"My mom," he said as he adjusted the rear view mirror. "She's a shut in and we can't afford—" He clammed up.

"I'm sorry to hear that," I said.

"Let's just get on the road."

CHAPTER 16

As they'd planned, Mike and Dalton were waiting in the parking lot at the train station when we pulled in.

Mike walked up to the car to get in and saw me. The look on his face said it all.

Jerk.

Hal got out of the car and shook Mike's hand. "Sorry about the car. I'm getting a new ride next month."

"Why's she here?" he said, cutting right to it. He wasn't hiding his contempt.

I opened the car door and stood up, but kept the door open, my hand on the handle. Obviously, he wasn't happy to see me. I had to make the whole story gel. "You're such a stubborn ass. If you'd've just listened, instead of breaking up with me. Again. God, how you can dominate a conversation." *C'mon. Go with it. Improv. You're the king of method acting, right?* "I figured screw it. I decided I didn't need your permission. I went right to Hal. And he's glad I did. Aren't you Hal?"

I didn't give him a chance to acknowledge. "This man is a sharp businessman, Mike," I said, pointing at Hal. "I gotta tell you. He's been running the numbers and looking at how to lower the cost of goods sold. Haven't you Hal?"

Making him feel like he'd look good in Mike's eyes would only help me. "He was already researching the mortality issue when I got there. We both figured that a few tips from a bird expert like me could make all the difference." I flipped my hair back, as though I were bragging. "Didn't we Hal?"

He finally nodded.

"So he's invited me along, so I can do my thing." I directed my explanation at Dalton. Mike, being my boyfriend, should know about my knowledge of birds. "I'll take a look at the birds, evaluate the conditions, their care, that kind of thing, and suggest some changes."

"Dude," Hal said, "I don't know about your personal stuff, but, uh, she seems like she'd be an asset, you know, with the birds and all."

Mike's eyes rolled from him to me.

Dalton rubbed his hand over his mouth, no doubt hiding a smirk.

I winked at Mike. "I know you're mad at me honey bunny, but you'll get over it. You always do." I gave Hal a big smile. "We're going to be a great team."

Mike glared at me through narrowed lids, for the briefest moment.

I rushed forward, wrapped my arms around him, and gave him a big smooch, then pushed out my lower lip. "Don't be mad at me." I hugged him close and whispered in his ear, "Thought you could push me out? Don't even think about doing it again."

A grin spread across his face. "How could I stay mad at my honey bunny?"

He squeezed me tight, then turned back to Hal and turned on the charm. "Great idea, bringing her along. Wish I'd've thought of it. Got myself so caught up in all the other ways you and I are going to make lots of money. Besides"—he stepped closer to Hal, lowered his voice—"you know how women can be. They get to yammering away. It slipped my mind." He backed up, raised his voice back to normal volume. "All right, let's do this thing."

Mike gestured for Dalton to get in the back seat behind me

and moved toward the other side of the car.

"He's not going," Hal said over his shoulder.

Mike eyed me, then turned to Hal. "Why not?"

"There ain't room."

Mike gestured toward the backseat. "Sure there is."

"I said there ain't room." He said it with authority. He was in charge.

That's a change. It was the phone call he'd made. *That's it.* Something had bugged me about it. His voice. He'd acted subordinate to the person on the line. And he'd said, *just two.* He was repeating what he'd been told. Just two people.

Oh my! Hal wasn't in charge of this operation. Someone else was. The person on the line. My brain buzzed back through every interaction, every word he'd said. He'd never actually claimed he was running the show. He just hadn't dissuaded us from believing it.

"Next time," Mike said to Dalton with a shrug.

Dalton nodded, all easy going about it. But I didn't like it. I didn't like it one bit.

Hal headed for the driver's seat. Mike got in the back.

Dalton looked at me, his eyebrows raised. He sensed I'd realized something vital.

"Okay, see you later then," I said, then mouthed, *Hal's not in charge.*

Dalton's eyes were filled with concern. Had he understood me? Or was he worried because he didn't understand?

I plopped down in the front seat and Hal pulled out of the lot.

We weren't even on the interstate yet when Mike started in. "So, honey, just so I'm clear, you took it upon yourself to go talk to Hal about what exactly?"

"See, babe, it's like I'm always saying. You never listen to me. I tried to tell you. Inventory is one issue, but Hal's got a mortality problem. It significantly raises his cost of goods sold."

"And, of course, you think you can help."

He was fishing for information.

"Well, honey, as I was explaining to Hal, owls are particularly prone to stress and that is likely the main cause of death. I'm sure with a few changes, we can keep a lot more alive and ready for sale."

"But you—"

"I know." I had no idea where he was going, but I had to get control of the conversation. "Like Jim is always saying, gluing feathers together isn't what matters in the taxidermy. It's knowing the animal, making them look alive. I've been working really hard at it. Not that you'd notice."

"Hey," Hal said. "I thought you two kissed and made up already."

Mike's lips pressed together. He sat back and crossed his arms.

I grinned at Hal. "And to think, you almost went without me."

Regardless of how I felt about Mike, I had to find a way to tell him what I knew about Hal. We might be walking into a hornet's nest. Or maybe... *Oh, my god! Could it be?* Could this be the importer Hyland wanted to bust? The whale she was after? It made sense. *Someone* was getting all the illegal game across the border. But they'd have to get it into Canada first, which didn't seem like it solved much. Canada's border patrol is as good as ours. But it wasn't out of the question.

Oh, my god! That is it! I'd been so blind. Of course that's why Mike swooped in to take over. He was going after the importer. And he thought it was Hal.

That meant I still had information that he didn't.

After two hours on the road, north into Michigan, Hal pulled off at a rest area. "Hey, we've got a long drive and I'm beat," he said. "We need to take turns driving. So, who's up?"

"I'm pretty beat myself," Mike said before I could.

"Fine, I'll drive. I've gotta pee first, though," I said. A chance to text Dalton.

"Yeah, me too," Hal said.

He pulled into a parking spot and killed the engine. "I need you to put your phones in the glove box."

Dammit. "What? Why?"

"A precaution," he said.

Mike and I both put our phones in the glove box and watched Hal lock it before I hustled into the ladies room.

When I came back out, Hal was still in the bathroom. I got in the car.

Mike growled. "What the hell kind of stunt are you pulling here?"

"Me? Want to explain to me why you lied? You said we needed more evidence before going to Hyland."

"I changed my mind."

"And you decided it was a good time to push me out, too?"

"Push you out? Who says you were in?"

"Are you kidding? I brought him to you. You didn't even know who Hal was before I introduced him to you."

"Are you saying I wasn't doing my job?"

"No. I'm saying—"

"Actually, I don't really care what you think. I'm the senior agent here. I call the shots. And this situation requires a certain level of experience. It's way more complicated than you're trained for." His expression turned cold. "It's out of your league."

Out of my league? My hair caught on fire. "So, I was good enough to figure it out, to get him to talk, to confide in you, but I'm not good enough to stay on the case?"

He huffed in annoyance. "Dalton warned me about you."

What? I pulled back from the sting.

"You're impetuous and reckless."

"Dalton wouldn't say that." *Would he?*

"I saw you myself at the paintball range. You rushed in."

"It was *your* idea."

He sat back. "What's it matter? Obviously, it's true. You're here, right now, in this car. Case in point."

"Yeah, well, I had insight you didn't have."

"*Yeah, well,*" he said, patronizing me, "that's what phones are for." He caught sight of something over my shoulder. "Now shhh."

Hal was headed back to the car.

"By the way," I said in a hushed tone, so angry I couldn't hold it back. "I know what you're really after." Mike's expression gave him away. "And guess what, Hal's not in charge. Someone else is the importer."

I enjoyed the look on his face. He hadn't considered that. "How would you know that?" he asked, his words dripping with sarcasm and disbelief.

Hal flung the door open.

I spun around and faced forward.

Hal got in, grunted something about the weird people who hang out at rest areas, and started up the engine.

I was glad he was back. I needed time to settle down. To think. Mike had pushed every button I had. I'd been close to crawling over the back of the seat to rip his hair from his head. *Impetuous. Reckless!* What did he know? *Out of my league.* What an ass. I was on the team, same as him. I'd earned my place.

"Wait a minute," Hal said. "You were gonna drive."

He pushed open his door, got out, and came around to my side.

I slid over to the driver's seat, slammed the car in gear, and sped out.

No need to worry about getting drowsy as we drove through the night. I couldn't sleep if I'd wanted to. With Hal's muffler sputtering and Mike snoring, I drove down the endless highway, chewing on the inside of my cheek.

After another three hours on the road, after I'd drawn blood and started on the other cheek, I started seeing signs for the Mackinac Bridge. I'd graduated from Michigan State University, then worked in the Upper Peninsula after I'd joined Fish & Wildlife, so I knew the state well.

I nudged Hal. "We're crossing the bridge, right?"

He grumbled an acknowledgment and went back to sleep.

The Mackinac Bridge is five miles of suspension bridge that spans the Straits of Mackinac, the water between Lake Michigan and Lake Huron. It's the only connection from the Lower Peninsula to the Upper Peninsula of Michigan, and on to Canada.

It was already dark and the bridge was all lit up at night. Wind whipped across the roadway from the west, sending snowflakes swirling about. Once we were on the suspended part of the bridge, I could feel it sway.

"Hey, you mind slowing it down?" Mike said from the back seat.

So he was afraid of the bridge? "It's all right," I said, enjoying seeing him squirm. "The bridge was designed to sway with the wind. As much as thirty five feet from side to side."

Mike's face went slack.

I changed to the inside lane, the one that was metal grate. The tires rumbled and the car shook. "But don't worry. We're only two hundred feet above the water."

His eyes grew a bit larger. I grinned.

Once on the far side of the bridge, I eased up to the tollbooth. Hal dug out his wallet, and handed me some cash. I handed it over without a word.

Hal had me pull into the rest area there and he took over once again at the wheel. Mike seemed to get his color back.

"Hal, you invited me at the last minute and, uh, I don't have my passport," I said, fishing.

"Don't worry about it," he said.

"But we're going to Canada, right? You said over the border."

"Don't worry about it."

About twenty miles up the highway, he took the exit to De Tour Village. There was a ferry there, I knew, that went to Drummond Island, the eastern most island in Lake Huron's North Channel that was U.S. Territory. The Canadian border was only five miles to the north and one mile to the east of there. Were we headed to the island? Was he taking us across the North Channel, in the dark of night, in January? I wouldn't put it past him. He'd said it was just over the border. On the north side of that body of water, there was a whole lot of wilderness. A lot of remote areas to hide or meet for illegal transactions.

In the summer, he'd make the passage by boat, but this time of year, the lake was likely to be frozen, which meant crossing on snowmobiles. I'd heard of the snow bridge, as they called it. After the holidays, when the water would freeze, locals would use their Christmas trees to mark the trail across the lake where the ice was safest.

Whether he crossed by boat or snowmobile, this remote area was a good location to avoid border patrol.

Several miles down the road, it was clear we were taking the ferry to Drummond Island. There was no other explanation for coming this way. It made the most sense.

At nearly three in the morning, we arrived at the ferry loading area. The wait was short, the ferry docked and we drove onboard. It was quite small, with room for about thirty-six cars. The passage was only one mile across, so the trip was quick.

Once we left the dock, the deckhand came to the car window for the fare, and we were already on the other side. Hal turned the ignition and drove off.

Another ten miles down the road, give or take, he turned north onto a snow-covered two-track that had been well used, the snow beat down to ice. We bounced through the woods to a fork, where he veered right, and continued on to the water's edge.

The winter had been quite mild this year, and the lake wasn't frozen. Ice chunks floated in the shallows, bobbing on the waves as they rolled to shore.

Tied to a rickety old dock was a bass fishing boat, an aluminum craft with a big outboard motor, the kind designed to skim across the water at fifty miles per hour. If we were going in that, it would be damn cold, not to mention dangerous, driving that fast across the water in the dark, dodging the chunks of ice floating out there. This guy was nuts.

I had on the fancy fur coat and a hat and gloves designed for fashion, not a forty-below windchill. "We're going in that?" I asked. "It's snowing and, like, fifteen degrees."

He looked to Mike. "Do you want to see it or not?"

"Of course," Mike said, annoyed with me.

Hal opened his trunk. "Here," he said and handed me a pair of Carhartt bib overalls. "Put them on."

Great. He was taking us across the lake.

It appeared to be the only pair he had. At least he was being a gentleman by offering them to me.

He slammed the trunk shut. "C'mon," he said and headed for the boat.

My eyes lingered on the glove box and my phone, locked inside.

The outboard engine fired up with one turn. That was a good sign, at least.

Mike and I climbed aboard, and Hal backed the boat through the ice chunks, out into the open water. He brought the bow around and hammered down on the throttle until the boat got up on plane, then throttled back.

Of course, he had no navigation lights on. At least I didn't have to worry about running into other vessels in the middle of the night in January. Even the freighters didn't run this time of year.

The icy wind whipped in my face. I wanted to turn around and put my back to the wind, but I couldn't bring myself to take my eyes off the water, where I might spot an iceberg that could send us headlong into the frigid waters of Lake Huron.

We zinged across the surface in what I figured was a northwesterly direction toward Saint Joseph Island, Canadian territory.

After about ten miles, my hands numb, my face without any

feeling left at all, Hal pulled back on the throttle, and brought the boat between two small islands offshore from the southern tip of Saint Joseph Island. He headed toward the west side of the eastern island, killed the engine, and let the boat float up onto the beach.

"Now we wait," he said.

It was still dark, the night sky filled with stars, the snow along the shoreline like a strip of glowing white.

Mike put his arms around me. "I'm sorry, honey bunny. You were right. I acted like an arrogant fool last night. Forgive me?" He nuzzled my neck.

He was trying to eliminate any sense of conflict for Hal. Or maybe he wanted to hug me for warmth.

"You know I could never be mad at you for long," I said, and rubbed his nose with my nose.

Hal shifted in his seat.

"So what are we waiting for?" Mike asked.

"We just wait," Hal said.

Okay.

Mike pushed on. "This is quite the route you've got. I assume we're already in Canada."

Hal nodded. "I told you it wasn't a problem."

"What about when the lake freezes?"

"Snowmobile. But that's the thing, another reason I need inventory in Chicago. I can't get across on the shoulder seasons in a boat when the ice starts to form, and I can't use a snowmobile when it's too thin."

"I see," Mike said, nodding. "And if you come for one or two birds at a time, you are making the trip a lot, increasing the risk of getting caught. Whereas if you could buy, say, ten or twenty at once, you could transport them in one trip."

"Exactly," Hal said.

"So, right now, we're waiting for...?" Mike asked.

"We just wait," Hal said again, shutting down the conversation.

The moon disappeared over the horizon as the eastern sky turned pink and the sun hinted at its arrival.

I managed to get a little sleep, off and on, leaning on Mike.

Finally, as the sun broke over the horizon, a low buzz grew in volume from the northeast. A plane. A little four-seater. With big, plump tundra tires for landing gear.

It circled, before coming down for a landing on the shoreline.

Hal turned to me and said, "Hope you're not afraid to fly," followed by a chuckle.

Little did he know, I had quite a harrowing flight in a bush plane in Alaska just a few months ago.

"How far are we headed?" Mike asked.

Hal shrugged. "It's in the middle of nowhere. He, my guy I mean, moves it around a lot."

That meant a pretty sophisticated operation. And to have use of a plane. This was no fly-by-night trafficker.

My nerves tingled with excitement. We were on the trail of something big.

CHAPTER 17

The pilot said not one word as he crawled out of the cockpit. He looked us over, probably assessing our weight, then confirmed with Hal that we didn't have phones, before he opened the door for us to get in.

I hung back, knowing that those entering first would have to get in the back seats. I wanted the front passenger seat, next to the pilot.

Hal and Mike got in the back without argument.

In moments, the propeller whirred to life and we bumped down the shoreline, took to the air, and headed north.

Below, the water sparkled in the morning sun. The pine trees along the shoreline, their branches dusted in white powder, blended in with the snow covered ground.

I looked at my watch. 8:10 a.m. Our flight speed was 120 knots, about 140 mph. At 8:15 we flew over the main east-west highway. A small, port town lay to the east. Probably Thessalon. Then the land was covered with thick forest.

About twenty minutes later, the plane banked right and we started a descent into a heavily wooded area. I scanned the ground, wondering where in the world this pilot thought he was going to land this bird.

We circled again and came down, landing on a narrow, but open stretch of land that must have been cleared as a fire break. There were no snowmobile tracks, no sign of any other way in or out, other than by air. If the birds were being held here, they were being brought in by air, too. Or captured near here.

The plane bounced, skidded, and came to a halt on the snow.

The propeller slowly stopped spinning, but the pilot didn't kill the engine. Either he wasn't staying long, or he didn't want to risk not being able to start the engine again.

When I jumped out of the door, my feet sank in the snow up to my knees.

Hal led us into the trees where a man, bundled in a thick black parka and a brown Stormy Kromer hat with the flaps down, met us, shotgun trained in our direction. He looked us up and down as though assessing whether we could hold our own in a wrestling match.

This man was the head honcho. There was no doubt. It was his plane. His set up. And he was making a clear statement.

Mike scanned the forest before approaching the man, his hands up and out to his sides. "I'm Mike. Nice to meet you…" He left the end of his sentence hanging with a question mark, fishing for a name.

The man gave a curt nod, letting Mike's hands fall back to his sides. "I've heard you're a tough negotiator."

Mike chuckled. "Yeah, I've been told that."

I plodded through the snow toward him. "I'm easy to get along with. Glad to meet you."

The man gave me an amused smile. "You want to see the birds." It wasn't a question.

Mike and I nodded in unison.

He used the shotgun to gesture in the direction he wanted us to go. He moved like a bear, slowly, but with purpose. I had the sense he could charge with the brute force of one, too.

At least the snow had been beat down into a trail here. I pulled the fur coat tighter around my middle. It was freezing out here. I was glad we wouldn't be here long. Confirm there were live birds and back to the warm plane.

Not fifty yards into the forest, the man led us to a spot

where several large, makeshift cages had been fashioned from stripped branches and chicken wire. They were about eight by ten feet, the sides about four feet high. Inside one, I counted twelve adult snowy owls standing on the snowy ground, white feathers scattered all over the pen. In the other pen, fifteen.

I stared at them, but I still couldn't believe it. He really had snowy owls. I'd been right about Hal. And here was the proof. Right in front of me.

Hal came up beside Mike. "See. What'd I tell you?"

My focus shifted to the man with the shotgun. The one in charge. I had so many questions. Who was this guy? Who caught the birds? And where? How did he get them here? How many had he sold? How fast was he selling them? Any of these questions would need to be asked very cautiously or could put suspicion on us.

Mike wasted no time, though. "So you're the brains behind all this?" he said to the man, then turned to Hal. "And you place an order somehow, phone, email, then you take the boat to that island and wait. And a plane drops off a bird. That how it works?"

"Pretty much," Hal muttered.

Mike turned to the old man. "How many can you deliver at a time?"

"Gotta box 'em," the man responded. "The boxes are like this size." He held up his hands to indicate dimensions, about the size of a shoe box. "You want to keep 'em immobile."

"So, as many as we can transport on our end? Say if we used a cargo van? Maybe fifty?"

The man nodded, considering. "We could probably put that many in the plane."

"And how does money change hands?"

"Cold, hard U.S. currency. Right then and there. No cash, no birds."

Mike nodded as though that was expected.

One bird hoppity-hopped, stretching his legs and flapping

his wings. Others stirred, pecked at him. That many predatory animals put together in one cage made for a dangerous situation.

"Keeping them together like that isn't a good idea," I said.

The man eyed me. "You some kind of tree hugger? They're fine."

"They're not fine," I said. "What do you feed them?"

The man gestured toward a canvas tent—army issue—pitched a little deeper in the woods. "Kyle takes care of it."

Kyle? I hadn't noticed the tent until now. How had I not noticed it? Did this Kyle live out here and tend the birds?

"You can talk to him all you want when he gets his ass out of the outhouse."

Right.

Mike plowed on. "How soon can we get these bigger orders coming?"

"Did you bring cash today?"

Mike laughed. "I've seen all I need to see." He turned to Hal. "You've got a deal. We'll give it a try."

Hal grinned.

We had all the proof we needed to plan a takedown. Mike would get the storage location set up as Hal had asked. They'd place an order, then Hal would make the pickup and we'd bust him as soon as his boat hit the shore. We'd also give the Canadians a heads up, coordinate everything with them so they could track the plane.

We'd done it. We were going to nail this guy to the wall.

But something didn't feel right. The old man was eyeing Mike. Had he agreed too easily? "I don't think that's such good idea," I said to Mike.

He turned toward me, frowned with annoyance.

"This is not the best way to house these birds. The trip here alone has been rough on them. Then to put them in cages together like that. Look how stressed they are. Then he's going to box them? How will you even know if you're buying a live bird? They could be dead already when you load them into the van." I turned to Hal. "Isn't that right? You said you were getting dead birds." I turned back to Mike. "Like more than fifty percent. That's an awful lot of money when another half are dead before they get to Chicago."

Mike calmly turned to the old man. "So, I'd get my money back then, right?"

"I send 'em out alive. No refunds. Your problem."

Mike seemed to ponder this. "I lose too many, I won't be coming back."

The old man didn't seem to care.

Mike smiled at the old man. "I'm sure it'll work out."

"Or, better yet," I said, "I could offer some tips, help you with the mortality problem. With just a few changes here—"

The man held up a fat mitten. "Talk to Kyle."

From down the path, here came Kyle, bushy-haired, scruffy bearded, clad in an army issue jacket.

He shuffled up to the group, yawned. "Yeah?" Then his eyes grew wide. "What the hell?" His eyes darted from the old man then back to Mike. "Mike Wessell?"

"You know this guy?" the old man asked, raising the shotgun.

"Know him? He's the bastard arrested me. He's a cop."

CHAPTER 18

Oh shit! "You're a cop?" I shouted, adding as much surprise and disgust as I could muster.

I shuffled away from Mike as fast as my fluffy boots would take me. Not only did I not want to get caught in the crossfire, but the only way to save him was to not get made myself.

Mike threw his hands up in the air. There was nowhere for him to run, not a chance of getting outside the range of that shotgun.

"You asshole!" Hal spat.

"Hal, you dumbass," the old man said. "You brought a cop here." He didn't seem overly agitated. He was rather calm, actually, like this was just another bad day at work.

Hal shook his head in frustration.

The old man was too far away for me to disarm him. I had to get closer.

"Now what are we gonna do with you two?" the old man said, holding the weapon steady.

Mike's face went white.

I had to do something. "Two? I'm not a cop."

His eyes narrowed. "You came with him, didn't you?"

"Yeah, so did Hal."

"I know Hal. I don't know you."

"That doesn't make me a cop."

Mike was smart enough not to say a word. Still stood there

with his hands in the air.

I had to make a scene. Somehow get closer to the old man, to that gun. I had to throw a fit. Stall. *Something.* "A cop? I can't believe it. I loved you, you rat!"

"Shut up," the old man said, bringing the shotgun around toward me.

He was quicker than I'd expected. I threw my hands up, too. "Don't point that thing at me!"

"Shut up!" The shotgun swung back toward Mike. "Kyle," the old man said over his shoulder, "go get your shit. We gotta bug out."

Kyle hung his head. He must have liked it here. But he hustled toward his tent.

"Hal," he ordered. "Get over here."

Hal shuffled closer to him. "Yeah?"

"You made this mess. You gotta take care of it." The old man held the shotgun for him to take.

Oh, my god! He was going to shoot us. My knees started to shake.

"What?" Hal stood there with a dumb look on his face.

"Hal, you don't have to do that," I said. "Don't kill him. There isn't anything that's been done that can't be undone. Isn't that right, Mike?"

Hal looked at me with terror in his eyes.

"It's your mess," the old man urged, pushed the shotgun at him.

Mike dropped to his knees in the snow.

My bowels churned like an old-fashioned washing machine.

Hal shook his head. "I ain't no murderer."

The old man sighed. Frowned.

"I suppose it don't matter no way to you anyhow. You're as good as busted. You're gonna have to vanish." He turned his attention back to Mike. "But as for me, well, I don't like loose ends."

Mike shook his head.

Keep him talking. "What's it matter?" I said. "He probably doesn't even have that, what do they call it, jurisdiction up here. We're in a different country."

The old man lost his patience. The shotgun swung back around, but this time he raised it to aim. Right at me.

My hands shot up higher. A bolt of fire sizzled through my digestive tract. "Shutting up. Got it."

"Kyle! Hurry up!" He yelled.

Kyle came running with a backpack on his back, snowshoes and an ax in one hand, and a plastic garbage bag swinging in the other. It must have been stuffed with something light. Sleeping bag? A shotgun and an army canteen were slung over his shoulder. A frying pan and small saucepan hung from his pack. He looked like Grizzly Adams.

He was told to get to the plane. "Tell him we're bugging out."

Kyle shuffled away.

"You, too, Hal."

My chance to move closer. "Wait up," I said to Hal and trundled after him, my head down.

"Not so fast," the old man said.

I halted in my tracks. *Dammit!*

"There ain't room in the plane for you."

"What? Why? I'll squeeze in the back. You can't leave me here."

If he meant to kill Mike, he wouldn't leave me alive, a witness to the murder. My hands shook. *Please don't let him see.*

"But you don't understand." I swung around. "Hal, tell him. I can help. With the birds." I looked right at the old man, took another step toward him. "That's the whole reason I came. See, I can save you a lot of money. Hal, he was telling me about the dead birds. The mortality rate. Just think,"—I took another step closer—"if you kept more birds alive, more to sell, right? More profit." I was rambling now, but it was buying me time. "A dead bird's not worth anything. You've lost your investment. I mean, I don't know where you got Kyle, but he's not exactly taking good care of the owls. You can't—"

"Shut up."

I sucked in a breath.

I was only ten feet from him now. If he swung the shotgun back toward Mike, I might be able to charge him.

"I tell you what. You go on ahead and take care of those birds." He smirked. "I'll stop back by in a few weeks, see how they're doing."

His attention turned to Mike, and with it, the gun. It was my chance.

I launched toward him. One step. Two. I slammed into him, knocking him off his feet. We tumbled into the snow in a heap. I got a grip on the barrel of the gun.

Boom! A shot blasted off, echoing through the forest.

It wasn't this gun. I cranked my head around.

Kyle stood twenty yards away, his weapon aimed at Mike.

"Get off of him or my next round goes in the cop's head."

I shoved off of the man and got to my feet.

He took his time getting up, brushed snow off his pants, then raised his weapon once again and trained it on me as he slowly walked backwards, toward the plane.

Hal seemed puzzled by the whole situation. "You leaving them here?"

"Unless you want to go directly to jail? I figured you'd like a head start to get your dumb ass outta Chicago."

His eyes fixed on me. "Gimme my overalls back, bitch," he said.

"You can't leave us. We'll die out here. We'll freeze to death." No way was I dying here. But putting the idea in his head might save our lives, seal the deal that he didn't need to shoot us.

Hal stormed toward me. "My overalls."

"Okay. Okay." I opened my silly fur coat, unclipped the shoulder straps, and pulled the bibs off. "Here." I tossed them at his chest.

He spun around and hightailed it toward the plane.

I pleaded with the old man one more time. "C'mon. At least drop us off somewhere. You can't leave us here with nothing to survive."

"Not my problem," he said, then grinned. "Best of luck to ya."

CHAPTER 19

The propeller roared to life and I watched, helpless, as the plane took off down the clearing then lifted into the air and was gone.

Relief washed over me. We were alive.

"You okay?" I asked Mike.

He stared off into space, his face still white. "I..." He closed his eyes, opened them again.

"You're all right," I said, moving toward him. "It's okay. We're okay."

He held up a hand, didn't want me to come any closer.

"What's wrong?"

He shook his head.

"Are you hurt?"

He turned toward me. His face turned from white to red in an instant. "What the hell were you thinking?"

"Me? What'd I do?"

"You gave yourself away when you tackled him."

"What?! Was I supposed to let him shoot you?"

"He wasn't going to shoot me. You had the opportunity to get away and come back for me. And you screwed it up."

"There was no way he was taking me back in that plane and letting me walk."

"You're a sorry excuse for an agent."

His words hit me like a thunderclap. I stepped back.

"Now we're alone. In the wilderness. In the dead of winter."
He crossed his arms in front of his chest. "We might as well
be dead."

"Yeah? Speak for yourself," I said, and headed for the tent.
Kyle couldn't have taken everything with him that fast. There
had to be some warmer clothes, coats, something. I needed to
get warmed up, then figure out what to do.

Mike followed. I didn't know him well, nor did I have
training in dealing with trauma, but I was willing to bet he was
in shock. I thought that man was going to shoot us. For sure,
shoot Mike. He must have thought the same.

An overwhelming dread came over me. The forest around us
was deathly silent. I pulled my coat tightly around my neck.
I was shivering. Not good. There was no doubt about it. We
were in a full-on survival situation. Our coats weren't insulated
enough for this kind of weather. We were fifty miles from any
form of civilization. And no one knew where we were.

We were on our own.

I'd spent enough time with Dalton to know that we had
to keep moving, keep focused. We couldn't dwell on what
happened, or what might happen, or the worst. We had to act.

I turned around to face him. "We can't argue about it. We're
here now, in this situation. We have to focus on what we're
going to do about it."

"There's no *we* in this scenario." He stormed past me.

Inside the tent, the air was warmer than outside. A fire
smoldered in a tiny wood stove.

Mike sat on the cot warming his hands while I went through
the few items that Kyle had left. There was an aluminum,
percolating coffee pot, a stack of Penthouse magazines, several
sticks Kyle had whittled to a point, probably out of boredom,
a stack of kindling for the tiny wood stove, though no matches
that I could find. Next to the wood stove was a blue, plastic
fifty-gallon drum, about one quarter full of water.

Outside the tent was a cookstove. Again, no matches to be

found. I'd have to make sure the fire didn't go out.

I'd hoped for extra blankets, but remembered that Kyle's sleeping bag had been tied to the top of his backpack. The bag he carried must have held any extra blankets he might have had.

I filled the coffee pot about half full with water. "Here, drink some water," I told Mike, holding it out to him.

He looked at the pot with confusion.

"It's all I can find right now. But you've had a shock. You need to drink."

He snatched the pot from my hand. "I'm fine. You're the one not thinking clearly."

"Nevertheless," I said through clenched teeth. "I'm going to get a look around, assess the situation."

"The situation is we're screwed." His hands shook.

"We're alive," I said. "And I intend to keep us that way."

He glared at me, but he looked like he was having trouble breathing.

All this bluster was a front. He was terrified. "Listen to me, Mike. Everything's going to be okay. We're going to be fine. Trust me."

"Well, aren't you the cute little optimist."

I shook my head and left him in the tent.

I circled the camp. There wasn't much else worth noting. Apparently, Kyle lived a simple life. He probably had no choice. If Mike had arrested him at some point, he was likely on the lam, living out here in the bush to stay out of sight. He must have had a food cache, likely up a tree. I'd need to find that soon.

I even checked the outhouse, which turned out to be a couple of wood pallets stood upright and stuffed with pine boughs to give some privacy. A medical potty chair with the bowl removed had been placed straddling two logs which spanned a hole in the ground. A smelly hole. A shovel leaned against the pallets. A plastic box held two rolls of toilet paper.

There was a woodpile, but nothing that we could use to start a fire, to cut anything, to signal for help. Just extra toilet paper. I could survive without that. "Thanks for nothing, Kyle!" I said out loud.

I circled back to the cages and the birds. There was no sign of anything to care for them. No food box. Nothing. Just the cages. Maybe there'd been supplies on the plane?

The owls became agitated as I approached, scurrying about the cage, running into the sides. One flew up and grabbed the chicken wire with its feet, then tried to let go again and got a toe caught, causing it to flip and fall to the ground. They were in a frenzy. If I opened the cage, they might attack me.

But I had to set them free.

The makeshift door had a padlock on it. *Seriously Kyle?* We were in the middle of the wilderness and he needed a padlock?

The chicken wire fencing was attached to the posts by strips of wire that had been wound and twisted. I couldn't find anything to cut the wire. I'd have to untwist every one of them. But it was so cold, even a few minutes with my hands exposed, I wouldn't be able to unwind the wire.

Back to the tent I went. I needed to check on Mike anyway. I wasn't sure the progression of the symptoms of shock, but it couldn't be good.

When I entered the tent, he was lying on his side, his knees pulled up to his chest. He quickly sat upright.

"There's got to be something here. Some scissors. Something," I said, pushing aside the stack of magazines, hoping to find any kind of utensil.

Mike lifted his head. "What do you need?"

"Something to cut the chicken wire. I've got to set the birds free."

He eyed me, considering something. Then, with reluctant surrender, he shoved his hand into his pocket and produced a Leatherman tool.

Relief flooded through me. This tool might save our lives.

"What luck!" I said. "I never thought of you as the kind of guy who'd carry one."

He shrugged. "My dad gave it to me. I've never used the thing."

He handed it to me. It was cold. Ice cold. It hadn't been in his pocket for long. He must have seen it before I did, as I was searching the tent, and taken it for himself.

Why'd he give it to me now?

I smiled, hiding my concerns. "Well, we have your dad to thank."

I warmed my hands at the stove, then opened the tool and pushed the pliers out for use, then headed back to the cages.

"I'm going to set you free," I said, clipping at the wire at a frantic pace. I got one side detached from the post, then I clipped along the ground at the second side. Once that was open, I pulled back the fencing. "C'mon out! You're free!"

The owls huddled in the corner, emitting a chorus of little chirps, while one brave bird stood in front of them, her wings held slightly out from her body in attack position. When I moved, she moved, keeping her body faced toward me.

"Go!" I said.

I pushed through the fencing, circled the inside of the cage, forcing them to move toward the center and the new door I'd created. Amid squawks and flapping wings, they scurried in different directions, bumping off each other, frantic. "Get out." I waved my hands at them. "Go!"

One leaped into the air, raised its feet and came at me, talons out in front. It latched onto my arm, digging its talons in through my fur coat. It kept coming, snapping, trying to bite me. I flung my arm and it let go. "Sorry!"

Another bird saw the opening and hopped toward it. Then he was out. Another followed. Then the whole lot seemed to realize, and with a flutter of white feathers, they rushed through the opening and were gone, scattering in different directions.

I ducked through the opening and headed for the other cage.

These owls were hopping about, to and fro, as if they'd seen the others escape and wanted out too. I clipped through the chicken wire, but this time, when I pulled it back, the owls rushed out in a blizzard of wings and feathers, without barely a sound. Amazing.

I spun around to watch them go. One lone bird had landed on a stump, not twenty yards away. It stared, those yellow eyes locked on me. The head pivoted around, as he took a good look at the area, then came back to me, as if to say, "Are you going to be all right?"

"Be free," I whispered.

The bird spread its wings wide and launched into flight. I watched as it disappeared back into the wild. Where it belonged.

The cache, at least the only one I found, had next to nothing in it. Some oatmeal, one can of baked beans, one can of stew, and a container of rice. Perhaps new supplies for Kyle were on the plane that just left, too.

I used the Leatherman tool to open the can of stew, then tucked it in my back pants pocket, under the long fur coat, before I entered the tent. Mike sat in the same spot, on the cot, his arms wrapped around himself to keep warm.

I stuffed some more dry wood into the burner, poured rice into the coffee pot with some water and set it on the stove to cook.

"Here's how I see it," I said. "That coffee pot is the only container I can find that will hold water. We'll use it to heat some food, eat as much as we can now, because once we get going, we'll have to eat what we have left cold, out of the can."

"What?" he said, his face all screwed up with disbelief. "Why would we do that?"

"Because we need it to carry water."

He still looked confused.

"Water is more vital than food. We can survive three weeks without food, but we've got three days max without water. "

He pointed at the fifty-gallon drum of water. "What do you call that?"

"Doesn't matter. We won't be able to carry it when we go."

"Go? Are you nuts? I'm not leaving here." He hugged himself tighter.

"It's our best chance at surviving."

"My ass it is. We're staying put. There's water. A stove." He gestured at the cans I'd set down. "Beans."

"There's enough water for only a few days. And we can take the food with us."

"We can melt snow. We have a fire." He said it as if he were in charge and I needed to stand down.

"Sure, but for how long? Waiting for what?"

He gave me that condescending look. "Hyland's going to send out the troops. They'll find us."

"How? When we left our phones in Hal's car, even we had no idea where we were headed. For all they know, we could be anywhere from here to the Yukon."

His expression faded a little. His hands dropped down next to his knees where he gripped the edge of the cot. "We'll signal."

"With what? Sure, we could build three fires. But how will we keep them fueled? Kyle took the ax. We have no idea what the flight patterns are around here. It could be weeks, maybe months, before anyone would see them."

"I'll take that chance," he said and crossed his arms. "I'm not going to listen to another word about it." He shifted on the cot. "Just because your mom's an admiral doesn't mean you're in charge. It doesn't mean you know anything about anything."

That stung. My jaw clamped shut. I clenched my teeth, tried to control my temper. "For your information, my mother's a surgeon. I learned to survive from my dad, a lowly civilian photographer." *And Dalton.*

I took a long breath. "And I'll tell you this: the town of Thessalon is fewer than fifty miles directly south of here."

"And how do you know that?"

"We flew over it. I clocked our time and speed until landing."

"In the plane?"

"Yes, in the plane."

His eyes narrowed. "How'd you know to do that?"

"I always like to know exactly where I am."

He cocked his head to the side and harrumphed. He'd had such faith in his character, in his acting skills and ability to convince Hal and the others he was one of them, he hadn't considered a plan B.

"Between here and there, we flew over several roads. We just need to get to one. In this terrain, I think we can cover ten miles a day."

"In that deep snow? No way." His face hardened. "You're delusional."

"I'm going to make some snowshoes for us."

He huffed. "With your magic wand?"

"With pine boughs and wire from the cages. I'll make them today. We'll eat the rice and stew, get a good night's sleep, and head out first thing in the morning."

He looked at the coffee pot on the stove, then at the can of beans, shaking his head. "They say to stay put. We can survive here. Out there, who knows. That's how people die. They get out of their element."

Man, he was a pain in the ass. "I agree. But the thing is, amid Chicago skyscrapers, knee deep in government bureaucracy, betrayed by my own team member, that's where I'm out of my element. But here. In the wilderness. I'll take these odds any day. I'm walking out of here. With or without you."

CHAPTER 20

I dragged pine boughs from the makeshift outhouse into the tent and collected all the metal wire I could from the birdcages.

"We're going to need to be cautious. The snow out there is corn snow," I explained to Mike as I laid out the branches.

He stared at me as if I'd gone mad. "Corn snow? Seriously? *Corn* snow?"

"It's named for the texture. It's snow that has thawed and refrozen. The point is, it's unpredictable in its ability to hold weight."

"Uh, huh. Great."

Three boughs would work best to craft each shoe, I decided. They'd be heavy, but give more surface area beneath our feet, and the three branches, side by side, would make for a solid base, wide enough for my boot. Once I had the main branches lined up, with the branch point facing forward, I lashed them together with the wire. Then I strapped some chicken wire across the top, wide enough for my boot to slip inside.

"These snowshoes are a work of true craftsmanship, if I do say so myself," I said, admiring them. "They'll be awkward, but they'll work."

Mike eyed the shoes with skepticism. "Where'd you learn how to make those, anyway?"

"I read about it in a book."

He smirked. "Well, I read a book on race cars. Doesn't mean

I know how to build one."

I checked the pot on the stove. The rice seemed done. I flipped the lid off, dumped the stew in the top and stirred it with a stick.

"You can't be serious?" Mike said, staring at the stick.

"Are you hungry or not?"

He pursed his lips together. This whole situation had him stressed to the max. I should have felt sorry for him. I mean, jerk or not, he did just face the wrong end of a shotgun.

"You need to look on the bright side," I said.

"Yeah, what's that?"

"I'm here. And I know how to survive in the wilderness. We're going to be fine."

"Yeah, so you say. You learned it from a book. Great." He shoved more kindling from the small pile we had into the stove then plopped back onto the cot.

The stew seemed warm enough. I dug some out onto the lid with the stick, then tipped it up to my mouth. Though it was beef stew, and I'm a vegetarian, I ate it. I had no idea when I might see protein again.

I dug out some more and held it out to Mike, my eyebrows raised.

He looked at the stew, but didn't reach for it.

"Haven't you ever been camping?" I asked.

"I grew up in New Jersey."

"Right." I shoved it toward him. "Eat."

He took the lid, sniffed at the pile of rice and stew, and scarfed it down.

The impact of trauma on the mind is an amazing thing. One minute Mike's snapping at me, the next he's sound asleep on the cot.

I slipped from the tent to make one last look around before nightfall.

And to pace.

There was no denying the gravity of our situation. We had to leave. We had to try to walk out. We couldn't stay and wait. Of that, I was sure. But it still wasn't an easy thing to commit to. It was cold out here. Damn cold. One mistake and it could be deadly.

My dad had trained me to survive, to take care of myself, under all kinds of conditions. But mostly, we'd lived in tropical locations. Winter, snow, below freezing temps—those were something new. But no matter. I'd take it as it came. I was getting out of here. Back to my life.

Back to Dalton.

I looked up at the stars. *Are you thinking about me right now?*

Was he worried? Had he followed us? Tracked our phones? If he had, that would only get him as far as northern Michigan. Then what would he do?

Oh, Dalton. If only you were here. I wouldn't be worried at all.

I'm getting out of here. I'm walking out of here. You watch me.

I pulled the coat tightly around my neck. "Well, I asked for it," I said aloud, to no one. "I had to work my way in. I couldn't let it go."

I turned to face south. "Hal, you bastard. You better run fast, because I'm coming for you."

I paced some more, then walked toward the empty birdcages. The moon cast eerie shadows on the icy ground inside, where the birds had trampled down the snow. The sight of it gave me an overwhelming feeling of desolation, a reminder of just how alone I was.

I drew in a long, deep breath of the cold air. "That's all right," I said. A declaration. The owls were gone. Safe. Free.

And I would be, too.

Sharing a single cot with Mike was a mistake. I would have gotten more sleep on the cold, hard ground. But no matter, morning was here.

I fashioned a back carrier out of chicken wire and straps from the tent for the can of beans and the coffee pot. I turned the fur coat inside-out to take the best advantage of the fur's insulating factors, a point missed on the ladies who were more concerned about so-called fashion.

In case we did turn back, I stuffed the last of the dry wood into the wood burner to keep the fire going, hoping there'd still be coals. Carrying a burning ember with us would be a good option, if I could've found anything to carry it in. But I'd turned up nothing that would work.

I'd done all I could to prepare us. It was time to get going.

Mike followed me out of the tent.

The snow squeaked under my feet. The air was crisp—I guessed about five degrees Fahrenheit. "What I wouldn't give for a wool cap and real mittens," I said as I lashed the snowshoes to my boots.

"Are you sure about this?" Mike asked. He lifted his pine bough snowshoe, examined it, once again, with skepticism. "Will these even work?"

"Sure they will. We just need to be careful with them."

He shook his head. "We don't even have good winter coats."

"It's all right. We don't want to work up a sweat anyway. That's a good way to end up hypothermic when we stop to rest. The key is to pace ourselves. This way, we keep ourselves warm as we walk."

I held up my arm and positioned my watch horizontally. "The sun rises in the southeast, sets in the southwest this time of year."

"What are you doing? You don't seriously expect me to believe you can tell direction with a watch?"

"In the northern hemisphere, if the sun is visible, you point the hour hand in the direction of the sun. Then bisect the angle between the hour hand and the twelve o'clock mark to get the north-south line."

"But there's no sun."

"You're right." I dropped my arm. "Not now. But it might yet show its face today."

"So?" He held out his hands. "What? We wait?"

I held up my hand to point. "Well, that's south. As we progress, we're going to designate waypoints as often as we can. Then when we do get a glimpse of the sun, we'll reconfirm."

He pointed in the direction I had pointed. "And how do you know that is south?"

"When we flew in, the pilot banked and landed in the direction of the wind, which was a westerly, along here." I indicated the marks in the snow from the landing gear.

Mike stared at me. Did this guy have any thoughts of his own? Or did he always get ahead on the backs of others?

I slipped my hand back into my glove and plodded south.

"Wait," he said.

I turned. "What?"

"I don't think we should go."

"We've been over this."

"Yeah, but—" He looked back at the tent, then to the south, worry creasing his brow. "Out there." He shook his head.

He was scared. "I understand," I said, trying not to sound as exasperated as I was. "I tell you what. You can stay, if you want. I'll send them for you." It wasn't a good idea to split up, but I could see now that his fear was going to be a big problem.

For a moment, he looked relieved. Then his eyes turned dark. "Leave the coffee pot with me then."

"You can drink right from the barrel," I said.

"Not if it's frozen."

"You can collect enough downed branches to keep the fire going until help arrives."

He flung a hand in the air. "There's water all around for you. You can eat snow."

"By that logic, so could you," I said, annoyed now. "But the process our bodies take to heat and melt the snow internally is too energy-intensive. You'd die of dehydration and likely hypothermia."

His expression changed. He believed me for once.

The coffee pot was the only thing we had to hold water. If we split up, only one of us could have it.

He stared, trying to make up his mind about something. Was he going to try to take it from me? Had I underestimated how much the trauma of being shot at had affected him?

"It's only going to take me two or three days, max, to get there. You've got enough water in the barrel," I said, trying to calm his fears.

He shook his head again. "You're going to die out there and leave me with nothing."

I shook my head. This wasn't helping the situation. "C'mon, come with me. It's best if we stick together. I know it's scary, but you'll have to trust me. We'll be fine. I've had training for backcountry survival."

He shook his head again. His eyes narrowed. Nothing I said was going to deter him. He took a step closer to me. "Hand it over."

He wasn't messing around. Something had clicked in his brain. Now I was his enemy. I'd read about this. Primal fear makes people do horrible things. He might end up backing down now, but I'd have to be wary of him the whole trek. "Mike, you've got fresh water in the barrel. I'll send help in a couple days." I took off, tromping through the snow as fast as I could.

"You come back here with my pot, you bitch!"

He launched himself at me. I spun on him as he reached for the pot.

"I don't think so, buddy," I said.

He grabbed me by the collar of my coat. I thrust my fists up between his arms and slammed them downward at his elbows, breaking his grasp.

"Let's calm down," I said, taking a step back, an awkward move in the snowshoes.

He lunged at me. I sidestepped with one foot, bent to the side at the waist, and shoved him in the other direction. He went down, face first into the snow.

"Try that again, and I'll give you a real reason to stay," I said. I took several steps away from him, out of his reach as he got back to his feet.

With an expression of defeat mixed with respect, he clambered back toward the tent.

"Take care of yourself," I shouted after him. "I'll see you in a few days."

The wilderness can be a dangerous place, if you don't respect it. And I wasn't kidding myself, I could die out here.

I'd read once, that in a survival situation, one of the best signs of a true survivor, is the ability to appreciate beauty. And I did. I couldn't think of a more beautiful place to hike today. This old-growth forest had been selectively logged, so the ground was open under the canopy of tall beeches and maples, with a few low, wetland areas of pines, cedar, and birches.

The air smelled of fresh pine, crisp and clean. A breeze rustled through the treetops, making the brittle, cold branches clack together in a woodwind tune. The dried beech leaves fluttered, making the sound of ruffling paper. My cheeks flushed pink as the cold wind brushed across my face.

Chickadees sang out the melody, "Hey, sweetie. Hey, sweetie." The calendar had clicked past the solstice, and the days were gradually getting longer. The birds were already thinking spring. A time of optimism. And I was optimistic.

I set a pace, not too fast. I needed to get there alive and in one piece. When wearing snowshoes, your stride and the way you place your feet helps with stability. Without walking poles, I had to concentrate more than I normally would on keeping my balance and be careful not to step on the other shoe.

I'd always had an uncanny sense of direction, but I needed to pay close attention. In the thick forest, it's easy to get turned around. People have a tendency, when lost, to walk in circles. I couldn't let that happen to me.

Not far into the forest, perhaps a mile and a half, I came across a deer run. Their hooves had beaten down a path in the snow. Beech leaves poked through, making it look like a long, brown-speckled trail amid a vast swath of white.

Should I follow the trail? Would it lead to water? No. I had water in the pot. Enough for a day. I needed to keep heading south.

I checked my watch. I'd been walking for about an hour and a half. My pace, then, must have been about one mile an hour. Though I couldn't be sure. Distance is hard to judge in the snow. It's also easy to overestimate when a route is difficult. But I had to keep track, and my own judgment was the best I had at the moment.

I continued on. My concerns shifted back to Mike. Shock isn't something to mess around with. If he kept warm, he'd be all right. But I needed to get help, and soon.

After another hour had passed, I came to an opening in the forest. A large, smooth patch of white snow with no trees, about a hundred yards across. A pond. Or swamp? Whichever. It was best to go around. It was also a good place to assess waypoints. I chose a unique clump of trees on the other side, from what I reckoned was directly to the south, then proceeded to skirt the shoreline. When I reached those trees, I'd head into the forest again.

Not far to the west, I hiked through a spot where cattails poked up through the snow, a sure indicator of the edge of a body of water. I continued onward.

The ak-ak-ak-ak-ak rattling call of a pileated woodpecker pierced the silence. I caught a glimpse of him, flying across the open pond, with the distinct bobbing flight pattern of all woodpeckers. He landed on a dead birch on the far side. His red head stood out like a beacon amid the muted colors of the winter forest. Ak-ak-ak-ak-ak, he called again.

A downed log was in my path. I decided it was a good place to sit for a moment and take a drink of water. I lowered my makeshift backpack, sat down, and took a swig.

I sure had gotten myself into a predicament. What if I didn't make it back?

No. Stop that thinking.

Dalton was going to be mad as hell. And he had a right to be. What had I been thinking? Once again, I hadn't followed orders. But I had information no one else had. He'd understand. I knew he would.

But I'd said harsh words. It wasn't his fault Hyland had sent him. It was Mike's. Because Mike had lied. But still. Dalton didn't deserve it. My stomach clenched. What if I never got to tell him I'm sorry?

Stop it!

I said out loud, "The moment I see you, the first thing out of my mouth, will be, *I'm sorry, Dalton.*"

I nodded my head to make it so.

I'd been so angry that day. And all he wanted was me. Finally, we were alone together. And what did I do? Ruin it being obsessed with Hal and angry with Mike and determined to stay on the case.

What I wouldn't give to go back to that moment, in that hotel room, right now.

"It's no good to dwell on it," I said. "Gotta keep moving."

With the pot in the back carrier and pack on my back, I set out again.

About three quarters of the way to the clump of trees, I had a strange feeling I wasn't alone. I stopped, turned around, and scanned the forest.

Across the pond, I spotted movement. Mike. He must have been following my tracks.

He caught sight of me and started hoofing it across the pond toward me.

"No! Don't come that way!" I yelled, but he had his head down, his arms pumping to catch me. *Don't overexert yourself, you dope. Don't sweat.*

Another ten yards, then another. He kept coming, full force toward me.

What was he thinking now? Was he coming for the coffee pot still?

A thunderous crack echoed across the pond. Mike came to a halt, his head up, his eyes on me before he looked down at the surface of the pond as it collapsed around him. In an instant, he plunged through the ice.

CHAPTER 21

Oh, no! Mike popped up, gasping, his breath coming in short bursts. The cold water was such a shock to his system; he was hyperventilating. He had to relax, or his panic would make it worse.

"Keep your head up. I'm coming! Don't try to get out." I kicked off my snowshoes and dropped the back carrier, then hesitated. If I fell through as well, we'd both die. I had no idea how thick the ice was between us. The best thing to do in this situation was for Mike to crawl out in the direction he had come. That ice had been thick enough to hold his weight. But if I ran around to approach from that direction, he'd be in the ice water that much longer.

I had to get to him, then haul him that way.

His arms were flailing about. He was in a full panic. "Just breathe!" I yelled. "Don't try to get out yet."

I dropped to my belly and crawled across the pond on my elbows and feet, as fast as I could, spreading my weight as far and wide as possible.

Mike thrashed at the edge of the ice, breaking more off.

"Calm down!" I shouted. "Just get your breathing! I'm coming."

His face displayed sheer terror.

"I can save you. But you've got to listen to me."

His eyes registered surrender. He started to calm. His

huffing slowed.

I circled around and got to the side he'd come in from and backed toward him, my feet about five feet from the hole.

"Use your arms, pull yourself up and out, as far as you can. Crawl out on your belly."

He tried, but slipped back into the water, the edge of the ice breaking off wherever he put his weight.

"Don't give up!"

He heaved himself up again and got his belly hooked on solid ice, puffing and wheezing.

"Now kick those feet! Kick hard!"

He did, but his hands kept slipping as he tried to get a grip on the wet, slippery ice and he was encumbered by the big, clumsy pine-bough snowshoes.

"You're going to have to get the snowshoes off."

He shook his head. He was giving up.

I inched closer to him. "Okay, grab my feet!"

A hand slammed down on my ankle and grabbed hold with a death grip. "Kick those feet!" I dug in with my elbows and tugged. "Kick those feet! Don't you dare drag me in with you."

The sound of splashing and ice breaking behind me spurred me on. "Don't give up."

I heard a thump and him moan. He was up onto the edge of the ice.

I shouted, "Turn and roll. Roll away from the hole."

He did as I said and got onto more solid ice. He lay on his back, his chest heaving.

"Don't quit now. Get on your belly and crawl like me. Follow me out."

With what little energy he had left, he was able to roll back over and do as I said. We crawled all the way across the pond to solid ground.

I spotted a nice, tall spruce with branches heavy with green needles. The ground was clear of snow underneath. I grabbed at the branches, as high up as I could reach, knocking the snow off so it wouldn't fall on top of us later. On my hands and knees, I pushed the snow into a pile, making a windbreak.

Then I helped him up and got the mangled snowshoes untied from his shoes. "Now, under the tree," I told him.

He followed my direction without question and crawled under the boughs.

"We need to get your wet clothes off."

He didn't argue. I helped him with his coat, and had to pull his shirt off like he was a toddler, as he shivered uncontrollably. His shoes were easy. I wrestled with his blue jeans as he thrashed like a fish. "Underwear, too," I said. Wet cotton could kill him right now. I tugged, and off came the underwear.

I wrapped my fur coat around him.

His coat, even though it was wet, had a fleece lining, so it had some insulating value. I rubbed it with snow, smushing it in to get any excess water absorbed, then I wound it around his legs. I pulled off my own socks and stretched them over his feet. Then I gave his wet clothes the same treatment in the snow before I hung them on the south side of the tree. Finally, I lay down beside him and snuggled up to him like we were two spoons.

"We need to get you warm," I said. My own body heat was the best I had to offer.

His teeth chattered and he shook, his cold body sucking from me what warmth I had left. When I started to shiver, I realized I needed to move, get more energy flowing. I got up.

"Can you curl up inside the fur?" I asked.

He nodded.

"I'm going to head back around to get my snowshoes and the food and water. I'll wear your coat."

"No. Don't leave me." He shook his head. "Don't leave me."

"You're going to be okay. I'm going to get the food. That will help warm you up. And I need to move to get my body warm again. Then I can warm you some more. Okay? I won't be long. It's not far at all. Just stay covered. But move your arms around, get some blood flowing."

He gave me a reluctant nod.

His snowshoes, especially the wire straps I'd made, were in poor shape. I had to untangle the wires, bend them back into shape, and re-attached them. They'd have to do.

I strapped them on my feet and set out, around to the far side of the pond.

Getting warm was a priority. And his clothes dry. There was no question; his life was in danger. I had to keep him from going hypothermic. But snuggling on the cold ground wasn't much help. But what else could I do? We were too far from the camp.

Dammit. Why'd he have to come barreling across that pond? Didn't he know better?

Once I arrived at the spot where I'd dropped my things, I switched back to my own snowshoes, hoisted the carrier to my back, then headed back to Mike, carrying his shoes.

Along the way, I passed the same patch of cattails and I remembered another important thing I'd learned—ripe cattail flower-head fluff makes great insulation. I gathered as many heads as I could, fluffing them out and stuffing them inside my jacket, the back of my pants, inside my boots. Then I stuffed in more for Mike. There were so many, I felt like the Pillsbury Doughboy.

When I got back, I had him sit upright and I fluffed out the rest of the cattail heads on the ground beneath him.

"Are you hungry?" I asked.

He nodded, so I used the Leatherman tool to open the can of beans. "Cold beans. Yay. But it's fuel." I handed him the can.

He tipped it up, took in a mouthful, then held it for me to take.

"No, you go ahead. Eat as much as you can," I said. "You need the energy."

His eyes held mine. He nodded.

I took the top off the coffee pot. "And drink some water."

His gaze held on the pot. "Thanks," he whispered. "For saving me."

"You would've done the same for me," I said.

He shook his head. "No." His eyes dropped to his hands and the can of beans they held. "I wouldn't have known what to do."

I patted him on the shoulder. "Eat the beans," I said. "Let's get you warm."

He downed the rest of the can, took a drink of the water, then we lay back down, cuddled together, trying to fight the cold that threatened to make this forest our grave.

We lay there, snuggled together, for a couple hours, interrupted every fifteen minutes or so by me getting up and doing some jumping jacks to produce more warmth, before Mike finally said, "I think I'm actually feeling warmer."

"That's good."

The wind had picked up, blowing snow across the pond in wisps of cottony white.

"It seems colder though," he said. "Am I imagining it?"

"No. The wind is picking up. But the good news is, your clothes will dry faster."

"Do you really think so? In the winter?"

"Yep. It's called freeze drying."

He laughed. A good sign.

"I'm serious. Actually, it's called sublimation, which doesn't require heat. Sunshine would be helpful, but we'll have to take what we can get. The wind will do it, although slowly. We're stuck here for a while. They might be dry enough for you to put back on in the morning."

He acknowledged with a nod, adding, "That's a long time from now."

"I know," I said, understanding his concern. Every hour we weren't walking south was another we'd need water, another we'd risk bad weather, another we were exposed out here in the cold.

"What about frostbite?" he asked.

"Don't worry. We're going to stay covered under this coat," I said, trying not to reveal my worry. With the wind picking up, frostbite was only one of the many things to be concerned about.

"So what's your story, McVie?" he asked, the charm back.

"I thought Dalton told you all about me." I felt the tinge of anger about what he'd claimed in the car, about Dalton saying I was impetuous and reckless.

"He said you were a class act, a little inexperienced, but a helluva an agent. He didn't tell me why you wanted to be one."

"He said that?"

"Said he wouldn't trade you."

A blush reddened my cheeks.

"I can see why," he added.

"That's not what you told me in the car on the way."

"Yeah, well." He shivered. "I was aggravated with you."

Did that mean Dalton hadn't said it?

"So, why did you want to be an agent?"

"Simple. I've always loved animals," I said. "I can't stand to see them hurt."

"Sure. I get that," he said. "But there are lots of ways to save animals."

"You sound like my mom."

"I'm just saying, law enforcement isn't for everyone. It's dangerous."

The image of him back at the camp, standing with his hands up, and me tackling the man with the gun came to my mind. "I know. It's—" I couldn't come up with words. "A calling, I guess. I get a lot of satisfaction from putting away the bad guys, knowing there is some justice in this world."

"I feel that way, too," he said, as if he understood where I was coming from. "Though, in our line of work it's all about the big picture."

"Now you sound like Dalton."

God, I missed Dalton. If he were here, this would be a completely different situation. He'd never do something so stupid as walk across a pond like that. If Dalton were here, we'd have those men back there hog-tied and the cavalry on the way.

If Dalton were here...

We lay in silence for a while, listening to the wind whistle through the trees.

"I'm sorry," he said, startling me. "For how I acted. Back at the camp."

"You were in shock, Mike."

"Yeah, well."

"It's all right."

"How'd you learn those moves, anyway? I came after you and I didn't know what hit me."

"Oh that? I spent some time in the Philippines when I was a kid. My dad taught me a lot of things, but he wasn't a fighter. He wanted me to learn to protect myself, so he took me to study with this old stick-fighting master."

"Stick fighting?"

"People ask me what art I studied. It wasn't a formal martial art, per se. It was a style of fighting, or self defense really, that was practiced among the peasants. They used sticks, knives, swords—whatever they had. For many years, it had been shrouded in secrecy. If you understand the history of the area, you can see why they didn't want to give away their advantage to any outsiders. But when I was there, the times had changed."

"And it was your dad who encouraged you to learn? He sounds like a great guy."

"He was." An image of my dad, smiling at me while I showed him a new move I'd learned, made me smile.

"He the one who taught you how to survive in the winter?"

"Sort of."

"What do you mean, sort of?"

"Well, we never really lived in a cold climate. But he did teach me. In a way. I was homeschooled, I guess you'd say. We moved around a lot. Sometimes we lived on base. Sometimes, when my mom was out to sea, we'd travel. I pretty much grew up living out of a backpack.

"One day, when I was, I don't know, about ten, he gave me an assignment to research winter survival. Then he quizzed me, hammering me with one question after another. That was his way. If I couldn't respond immediately, it was back to the books. I studied the Inuit and their ways. The Shackleton expedition. The lives of the Sami of Norway. It's amazing how the people of the world have adapted to their environments."

"So, you've never actually been in a winter survival situation? Never trained in one?"

"Unless you count walking to class in January at Michigan State."

Mike threw his head back and roared with laughter.

The forest grew dark. Soon, I couldn't see across the pond. Then it was night. I was exhausted.

"I don't want to sleep," Mike said. "What if I don't wake up?"

"That's an old wives tale," I assured him. "Get some rest."

When his breathing slowed to a regular rhythm, I was finally able to sleep.

I awoke with a start. It was still dark. Something wasn't right. I sat up and pushed my head through the pine branches to listen.

In the distance, wolves howled, their mournful voices calling for others of their pack. There were three distinct voices. One started, a long arrr-ooooo. Then a second joined in, a higher pitch. The third added a baritone. The first broke into a yip-yip, and then started in again with a long, drawn out howl, the tone warbling up and down.

I nudged Mike as I snugged back under the coat. "Hey, listen to that."

"Wolves?"

"Yeah. Isn't it beautiful?"

"Beautiful? Aren't they on the hunt? What if they find us here?"

"They don't howl when hunting. That wouldn't be very stealthy. They howl to communicate, like to call the pack together. Or they might already have a kill. Don't worry. We're not in any danger. Besides, they sound like they're at least a half mile away."

"Not far enough," Mike grumbled.

"We're fine," I said. "Go back to sleep."

I lay still, listening to the ancient sound, feeling at one with the forest and all the living creatures. Cold or not, it was home.

We would be all right. In the morning, Mike's clothes would be dry, and all would be well again. We'd head south, to safety.

CHAPTER 22

When I woke, dawn was barely lighting the eastern sky, yet the forest glowed with moonlight reflecting off the snow. I crawled from under the tree branches and stretched. Big, fat snowflakes tinkled down from the darkness above. The air was crisp. When I drew in a deep breath and exhaled, a tiny white cloud formed in front of me.

"I can see my breath," I said to Mike. "Whew, is it cold. Up and at 'em."

"Are my clothes dry?"

I handed them through the branches to him. "Hurry up. I'm freezing. I want my coat." I moved from one foot to the other, rubbing my hands together, trying to generate some heat.

After I resorted to jumping jacks, he emerged, all dressed and ready to go.

"Shall we go around the pond this time?" I asked, wrapping the fur coat tightly around myself.

"Very funny."

I strapped on the homemade snowshoes and headed out, setting the pace. Mike followed.

The wind came at us out of the west. Good to know. I'd make sure to pay attention to any wind shifts. It would help with navigation. Though, in the thicker forest, it was hard to determine wind direction.

I chose to skirt the west side of the pond, so the forest would provide a wind block, and headed for the same clump of trees I'd decided to get to yesterday.

Mike followed dutifully behind, the swoosh, swoosh, swoosh of his pine-bough snowshoes assuring me he was still there.

"From here, we'll head directly south," I said when I arrived at the trees.

Mike didn't question. He simply put his head down and followed.

I pulled the collar of the coat snug around my neck and onward we went, trudging forward, into the thick forest.

Soon, the snow began to come down harder. The wind picked up.

Amid the trees, it was cold, but bearable. We only had to make it a few more miles. There had to be a road.

We came across another pond. This one smaller. I chose a tree on the south side to head for, then turned west to make the trek around.

Mike still said nothing.

"Are you warm enough now?" I asked. "Got the blood pumping?"

"Yeah," he said. Nothing else.

A part of me felt for him. Plunging into an icy pond must have been terrifying. He'd had quite a scare. And he was out of his element, having to put all his faith in me. And he hardly knew me.

The breeze swirled my hair in front of my face.

If we could get a few more miles behind us, we were sure to cross a road. We had to keep plugging along. One foot in front of the other.

Gusts of wind whooshed through the treetops, causing branches to bend and whip back. Snow fell from the trees in sheets on the wind.

"The wind's picking up," Mike said.

Yeah, tell me something I don't know. Just keep walking.

"And the snow's really starting to come down."

No kidding. I picked up the pace.

Snow whirled around me now, sticking to my face, tickling my skin. My hair whipped in different directions. I tried to tuck it back into the collar of my coat, but then another gust would yank it out again.

My face was numb with cold. I couldn't feel my ears anymore.

It was time to take another bearing, so I could confirm we were still walking south. I came to a halt. The snow was falling heavily now and as I peered through the woods, I had to concede that the sight distance had been greatly reduced.

That was one of the dangers of traveling in the snow. If there is bright sunlight on the snow, objects seem much nearer than they are. But if visibility is poor, during snowfall, and the colors are all muted together, then objects seem much farther away. In a blizzard, you can't see anything.

"We should stop and rest. Wait for the snow to lighten up," I said.

Mike came up beside me. "What if it gets worse?"

I didn't wanted to say it, but I had the same concern.

The forest seemed to close in on us. The wind roared through the treetops, knocking snow to the ground in a deluge of white.

I checked my watch and figured by the time spent, we'd hiked about three miles. We weren't making much progress.

"Let's just sit for a minute," I said.

We found a downed tree, brushed the snow from it, and sat down with our backs to the wind, then shared what was left of the water in the coffee pot. I scooped some snow into the pot. If I hung it on my back again, with the chicken wire, it'd never melt. I'd have to carry it inside my coat, against my body. That would be mighty cold. But there was no guarantee we'd find water along the way. Best to bear it.

I covered my face with my hands, trying to get some warmth back in my cheeks.

"Maybe we should go back," Mike said.

I sat upright, looked him in the eyes. "No. Nothing's changed."

"Besides this blizzard?"

"Okay. Fine. But here's the thing. In all survival situations, there is a rule of three. Most people know about S.O.S., three dots, three dashes, and three dots. Build three fires. You can go three days without water. Three minutes without air. All that. But one of the most important rules is taught by the marines. That's the rule-of-three decision-making process. You and I need to come up with three different solutions or, I should say, three different decisions. Then we choose one and commit to it. You with me?"

He nodded.

"Okay. One, we go back. Two, we go forward."

"What's three?"

"Three, is, I guess, we stay right here until the snow stops."

"Okay."

"We need to think through each scenario." I looked back in the direction from which we had come. "Our tracks are getting covered by new snow right now. If we go back, we risk getting lost. And even if we don't, and we find the tent again, we're back in the same predicament."

He nodded.

"We already decided the odds weren't good for us there."

"You did."

"Yes. And I was right. Another rule, by the way, is not to second guess. Fatigue, hunger, all that causes us to think less clearly. Second guessing gets people in worse predicaments."

"All right," he said, nodding that he conceded.

"If we go forward in this blizzard, we might lose direction and get really lost."

He nodded emphatically at that.

I held up the empty coffee pot. "If we stay here, we use up more hours that we'll need water."

He nodded some more.

"Well, what do you think?" Didn't he have an actual opinion?

"I think you're right. Whatever you decide, I'll follow you."

Well... thanks?

The snow was coming down harder. I glanced in the direction we'd been heading. I couldn't see farther than twenty feet away.

"We're staying." I sighed. "For now."

My watch read 2:00 p.m.

The wind settled for a brief moment and big, fat snowflakes gently fluttered from the sky. I stood, mouth open, and caught one on my tongue.

"What are you doing?"

"Catching a snowflake. Haven't you ever done that?"

"You're nuts. You know that?" Mike said.

I plopped back down on the log. "It's beautiful out here. Might as well enjoy it."

"You really aren't afraid, are you?"

"Well, depends what you mean. I have faith in myself and my ability to get us to safety."

"How can you be so sure?"

I shrugged. "I'm not. What I do know is that I won't give up. And that's what makes me a survivor."

He looked down at his hands. "Why'd you help me?"

"When? When you fell through the ice?"

He gave a slight nod.

"Well, what was I going to do? Let you drown?"

His bottom lip pushed upward with a subtle shrug.

"Because of the coffee pot thing? You were in shock. I told you that. You just got shot at and—"

"No. Not that." He tried to look me in the eye.

"You mean how you took over my case? Claimed you'd done the work? Yeah, that was pretty shitty."

He thought for a moment, and said, "You're young. You're still green. I have more experience and I thought—"

"It was still shitty."

He gave me a slight nod. That was all the acknowledgement I was going to get.

My dad once told me, one of the hardest things in life is to forgive someone who isn't sorry, and to accept an apology that's never given. Mike had betrayed me. There was no other side to the story, no mitigating circumstances. He'd stabbed me in the back for his own gain. He deserved my anger. But I also knew, how I dealt with him now, was a reflection of my own character, not his.

"The way I figure it," I said, "we're all human. We all make mistakes, do things we regret. It's what we do about it that matters. It's how we make amends."

He gave me another slight nod, his eyes on his feet.

"I couldn't leave you to die in the pond. Not when I could try to save you. What would that say about me?"

"Well, I wouldn't have blamed you."

"I would have." I turned to face him. "I want to know something though. When I introduced you to Hal, that's when you realized he might be the importer Hyland is after, right? You thought he was a much bigger fish and that's when you made the decision to take over, right? "

"He claimed flat out that he had a way over the border."

"I understand. But that's when you decided to push me out."

He shifted on the log, looking down. "I saw right away that the situation could be much bigger than one guy selling owls."

I nodded, giving up. No matter how I asked, how I phrased it, how much I prodded, he wasn't going to admit that taking over my case the way he did—like a bull with his eyes on the red flag, trampling everything in his path—was wrong.

The man seemed broken to me. What had made him this way? Willing to so easily befriend me, then take for himself what he hadn't earned? Where was his conscience? I'd been so angry. But now I saw a pathetic creature, one without the courage or strength of character to give me a simple apology.

If he did, it'd mean he was admitting what he'd done was wrong and he couldn't do that. He couldn't face himself in the mirror. Sad.

I suppose Dalton was right. I'd learned something about Mike. It was information. And in the future I'd make different choices. I'd learned a lesson about trust.

The wind kicked back up. We sat close together for warmth as my watch ticked the minutes away, then an hour, then another, all the while the snow blew around us in a fury. Several inches of fresh snow lay on the ground and it wasn't showing any sign of letting up.

"It'll be dark soon," I said, checking the time. "We need shelter for the night."

"Sure," Mike said. "I'll call for a booking at the nearest hotel."

Walking around to find some kind of shelter wasn't a good option. I dropped to my knees and started pushing snow into a pile.

"This is good, damp snow."

"Great. You gonna make a snowman now?"

"No," I said. "We're going to make a snow cave to sleep in. And you're going to help."

"You can't be serious."

"On your feet."

He did as I said and soon we had a good pile of snow gathered.

"Actually, we're making a snow wall to block the wind," I told him. "Let's pack it down hard, but get it as high as we can make it."

Once we were done, we lay down with Mike's back against the wall, mine against him, and I pulled the pine-bough snowshoes over our heads and leaned them on the wall at an angle to cover our heads and keep new snow from falling on us.

"Another thing you learned from a book?" he asked.

"Yep."

"If we survive this thing, I think I'll donate to the library."

I grinned. "Good idea." I pulled the collar of my coat up under my head as far as I could. "Try to get some sleep."

"Yeah, right."

Exhaustion took me.

When I awoke, the sun was up, but the blizzard hadn't relented. The snowshoe ceiling I'd made held a lot of weight in snow, bending in the middle, but it was holding. I crawled forward and peeked out. Snow was coming down so hard, I couldn't see twenty feet.

"We're stuck here for a while," I said, trying not to sound worried. My toes were numb with cold and my stomach ached. I hadn't eaten for two days now. I needed calories to keep warm and to have the energy to walk out of here, but we had nothing. I could forage, if the blizzard stopped. There were edible items in this forest, if one knew what to look for. But my head was a little foggy, and my memory wasn't the best. Making snowshoes was one thing. Finding and recognizing the right fungus was another. Besides, it would take time that would be better spent heading straight toward a road.

Mike groaned. An hour passed. Then another. The snow still didn't let up. Twelve to fourteen inches of fresh snow must have fallen since we'd crawled into the shelter. Walking with the snowshoes was going to be much more difficult.

For now, we were at risk of boredom and worry combining to cause bad decisions. We had to keep our minds occupied. I said to Mike, "The other night, when we had dinner, you gave me such a brief summary of your life. Tell me more. Like how an F.B.I. drug enforcement agent ends up on an animal issues task force."

"It's not much of a story really," he said. He'd been needing a change, and his boss was happy to make the recommendation. I wondered if it had anything to do with the way he treated his teammates.

We lay there against the snow wall for several more hours, him talking, me asking more questions to pass the time.

Finally, the snow seemed to lighten. I checked my watch. Five-thirty p.m. It would be dark again soon.

Mike grabbed my arm. "Did you hear that?"

"What?"

"A snowmobile. I'm sure of it."

"Which way?"

He scrambled out from under the shelter, stood up and pointed. "Quiet. Wait," he said, straining to hear.

I didn't hear anything.

"That way. It's the way we were heading. Let's go."

"Are you sure?" I asked.

"I heard it. Let's go."

I pushed up from under the shelter, using my force to knock the snow from the snowshoes. As I stood up, I nearly passed out.

"You okay?" He asked.

The world spun around. "Head rush. I stood up too fast is all."

"And you haven't eaten."

"I'm fine." My vision got blurry.

"You're not fine." He grabbed me by the arm and held me up.

"I just need... a second." I plopped down in the snow. Everything went black, and then slowly came back.

"We need to go now," Mike urged. "C'mon, I'll help you."

"No, no." I shook my head. "It's getting dark soon."

"It wasn't that far away. Listen to me." He shook the snow from my snowshoes and set them in front of me. "You said not to second guess, that we should trust decisions made when we are thinking clearly. Well, I'm thinking clearly. I've eaten, remember. Thanks to you. And I heard the snowmobile. No question. You have to trust me."

"But I'm not sure which way."

"I am," he said. "Now, get the shoes on."

He helped me up, and then kneeled down to strap my shoes to my boots while I held onto his shoulder for support.

"Just follow me," he said.

I glanced at my watch. We didn't have much time before it would be dark.

The wind whipped around me, icy cold on my face. I put my head down and forced one foot in front of the other, following Mike's tracks.

In fifteen minutes, we burst from the forest onto a two-lane road. I couldn't believe it. We'd been that close to a road!

I looked both ways.

"Someone's got to come along sometime," I said.

Mike paced. I checked my watch again.

Ten minutes later, headlights appeared out of the dusk. We stood in the middle of the road, waving our hands.

An old pickup truck eased to a stop. The driver rolled down the window. A woman, in her late sixties, wearing a purple knit cap with a silly pom pom ball on top, stared at us in disbelief. "You gone and lost your senses?" she asked. Then her gaze caught on our feet. "You donc strapped tree limbs to yer feet?"

"We're U.S. Federal officers," Mike said. "Could we get a ride please?"

"Well, I'll be. You're them two they been looking for." She waved us to the passenger side. "Get on in and get warmed up."

CHAPTER 23

The woman, Gladys was her name, drove us straight to the Thessalon Fire Hall. She claimed there'd been a search and rescue party forming before the blizzard came. "Helicopters and all," she said, throwing a lever to get the heater running full blast.

Mike and I held our hands in front of the vents, luxuriating in the glorious heat.

"What were you doing out there anyway? And dressed like that?" She shook her head, tsk tsking.

I didn't have the energy to explain.

"Uh, that's classified," Mike said.

"Ooooh," she said, nodding, a grin creeping across her face.

She drove right up to the front door of the fire station and left the engine running as she led us inside.

"I found 'em," she announced with pride. "Right here. These are them officers you been looking for."

Two firemen rushed forward, talking at once, asking if it were true, if we were all right. One veered off to grab a couple of folding chairs. "Sit, sit," he said, scraping the chairs across the floor and flipping them open.

I collapsed in the chair. "I'd like some water, if you wouldn't mind."

"Of course!" He shouted to someone in the back to bring glasses of water. "We've been worried sick about you. Got the search and rescue units all the way from Toronto."

Mike gulped the water they brought him.

"Take it easy," the fireman told him.

"How'd you know about us?" I asked.

"Your man showed up and he wasn't taking no for an answer, I can tell you that. He was shouting orders like he ran the place. Well, here he is now."

I spun around to see Dalton, running across the fire station toward me. I shot up from the chair and I was in his arms.

The exhaustion caught up with me all at once. My head got dizzy and my legs buckled. He held me up—solid, safe in those arms. "You're all right," he murmured in my ear. "You're all right."

"I'm sorry, Dalton. I'm so sorry. I love you and I didn't mean…" The room spun around me and went dark.

"Can we get her some juice?" Dalton said as he sat me down in the chair.

Then there was a cup of juice being held to my mouth. "Take a sip," someone said. "You're dehydrated and your blood sugar is low."

A nurse?

My eyes focused close, then slowly farther away. Dalton was across the room, his phone held to his ear, his eyes on me.

I turned to my left.

Tom was here, talking with Mike.

"I ain't never seen anything like it," he said in a hushed tone. "Even I thought he was going to kill him. Did you know he was a SEAL?"

Mike's eyes met mine and he pulled away from Tom. "You all right?"

I nodded.

"You're here, too?" I said to Tom, still feeling a little confused.

He nodded. "Dalton called right away and I picked him up. We followed you in the van."

Dalton walked toward me, his phone at his side. He crouched in front of me. "How are you feeling?"

"Okay, I guess. Just a little light headed."

"Hyland's going to call in a minute on their main line."

He helped me to my feet and we moved to a conference room.

The phone rang the moment I sat down.

"Glad you are safe and sound," Ms. Hyland said. "How are you feeling, McVie?"

"Just fine, thanks. A little low blood sugar is all. Nothing a cup of soup won't fix."

That brought a chuckle.

"Well, Mike you'll be disappointed to know, that due to the circumstances, we made the decision to call in all our officers and go ahead with the take down yesterday. Twenty seven simultaneous arrests."

"I understand," Mike said, surprisingly indifferent.

"We are already gleaning some valuable intel. All paths seem to point to a customs employee in Miami. We've called the F.B.I. to assist our agents down there. We should have more news within the week." She paused. "Though, it seems we have another importer to go after in Canada. Great job, Mike. You had good reason to suspect this Hal character."

"Yeah, well." Mike looked at me. "I wasn't clear in that meeting last week. What I meant was, I felt there was enough information to go on ahead and investigate, but uh, what I didn't mention was it was actually Poppy who suspected Hal."

I looked at Dalton. He winked.

"That true, McVie?" Hyland asked.

"It was a team effort, ma'am."

"Considering the situation," she went on, "we obviously had probable cause to search Hal's apartment and office. I sent a detective over this morning, but, unfortunately, we found nothing. So, unless you've got something—"

"Just our word against his," Mike said, his frustration loud and clear.

"We've had him in custody, but if there's—"

"What?" I asked. "What do you mean? He's in custody?" I turned to Dalton. "You caught him? But I figured he was in the wind. He left us two days ago."

"Didn't Dalton tell you?" Ms. Hyland said. "He and Tom followed you. He was concerned about the situation. Then, when your phone signal didn't move from the car, they staked it out. Then when Hal came back alone, well, I'll let Dalton tell you the rest."

"But you didn't find anything at his house? Or his office? No evidence to prove he was selling owls?" I couldn't hide my disappointment. Now, we knew for sure he was trafficking in owls, but we had no proof, no evidence to present to a judge. It would be mine and Mike's word against his.

"Not a thing," she said. "We're going to have to let him go."

"But—" *Argh!*

"That's the law. We can't hold him any longer. Dalton, make sure he's released this afternoon."

She hung up.

I dropped my head in my hands. I was so hungry, so tired. My head ached. "Wait!" I snapped to attention. "Call her back. Call her back!"

"What is it?" Dalton asked.

"Just call her back."

He grabbed the phone and dialed. In a moment, she was back on the line.

"Ms. Hyland. Hal has a mother. In Chicago. She's a shut in. She lives in a little three-flat, with a garage. I bet that's where we'll find the sales ledger he mentioned, and other evidence."

"Did you get her name?"

"No, but—Tom can you bring up a Chicago map? On your phone?—Just a moment." I scrolled around, following the route we'd taken when we left his office. "Here. Right here." I gave her the address.

"I'll call the judge right away and get a detective over there. Good work, McVie. I'll let you know."

I yawned. Sleep. I needed sleep.

Dalton rose from the chair and took me by the arm. "Will you lie down? I'll wake you the moment we know anything," he promised.

"Dalton?" I said, as he walked me to the cot. "You called in the rescue teams. You knew where we were. About, where we were."

He nodded. "If it wasn't for the blizzard, I'd have been out there looking for you myself."

"And you got that information from Hal?"

He looked down at his hands, and then raised his eyes to meet mine.

"But had nothing to charge him with. He had no incentive to tell you."

The edge of Dalton's lip curved upward.

Realization dawned for me. "What'd you do to him?"

Dalton woke me with a kiss on my cheek. "Wake up," he whispered. "I have news."

I sat up on the edge of the cot, bleary-eyed.

Tom and Mike came up behind him.

"Hyland called. You were right," Dalton said. "Hal's mother's garage was loaded with all kinds of evidence. The sales ledger. Identifiable feathers. Enough to arrest."

A warm sense of relief came over me. I looked to Mike. "We've done it."

He nodded.

Dalton added, "Oh, and she said for us to hurry up. Apparently we're needed in the Bahamas."

"Are you serious?" I asked, incredulous. "Don't tease me with sunshine right now."

"Dead serious. Something's happened with some dolphins.

Let's get Mr. Gruba booked and hop a plane, shall we?"

I liked the sound of that. "You said he was being held somewhere?"

"Back in Michigan. In the Chippewa county jail."

I turned to Mike. "Well, there you have it. You can go make the arrest."

Mike shook his head. "He's all yours."

Dalton tried to contain a grin, but only I noticed.

Tom's mobile taxidermy van only had room for two passengers, so he took Mike and a rental car was brought in for Dalton and me.

As soon as we were alone, I burst, "I'm so sorry for what I said."

"About what?"

"About you, getting to go, without me, and—"

"That's been bothering you? All this time?"

"Well, yeah."

He took my hand in his and held it tight. "I knew you didn't mean it that way. I haven't given it another thought."

"Yeah, but—"

"But nothing. All that matters is that you're okay. You had me worried."

"Yeah?" I smiled at the thought that I meant that much to him.

"Yeah." He squeezed my hand. "So, tell me the whole story. From the beginning."

I did, from the moment Hal had walked in the door at Wilson's. "I really learned some big lessons," I said.

"Oh yeah," he said. "Like what?"

"Like who I can trust and who I can't. Like how I tend to leap first, think later. But most of all, I learned something about forgiveness."

"What's that?"

"I used to be one of those eye-for-an-eye people. Betray me and I'll get my revenge, you know. But life's not that simple.

People and relationships are complicated."

He nodded in understanding.

"In the end, I feel good about myself for how I handled things with Mike." I looked at him. "As far as surviving, well, it was thinking of you, knowing you'd be waiting for me, that got me through."

He smiled. "I'm glad."

At the next drive, he pulled the car over to the side of the road, threw it in park, and took me into his arms. "I'm so glad," he whispered. "I'm just, so glad."

"Did I...? When I first got to the firehouse, did I...?"

"Say you loved me?"

My face turned red.

"I'm sure Tom heard you say it."

"Oh no."

"Don't worry. He won't say anything. He's a good guy."

I nodded.

"Besides, you were out of it. Delirious. I mean, you were exhausted. You weren't making any sense at all."

"Yeah."

He stared into my eyes. Then hugged me tight again. "I'm so glad you're safe."

Hal cowered in the corner of the cell. His eyes looked sunken in his head, and he twitched like a dog who'd been beaten. But there wasn't a mark on him.

Of course, there wouldn't be.

The young officer at the jail opened the door for me.

When Hal saw me, he shrank back even more. "Oh, God! Oh, thank God! You're alive." He shuddered.

"And guess what. I really am a cop."

"Oh, my God. I can't go to prison." He curled into a ball. "I can't go to prison."

"You don't have to," I said.

He snapped to attention. "What?"

"We want the man in Canada. And you're going to help us get him."

He stared, mouth agape. Then words came in a flurry. "No way. That's crazy. He'll kill me. I can't do it. No way."

I held up my hands, cutting him off. "You have the right to remain silent."

Author's Note

Thank you so much for reading and supporting this indie author. I can't tell you how much it means to me that you are enjoying my stories, and that the two of us can vicariously bust the bad guys who harm animals.

This story came right out of the headlines. In 1986, U.S. Fish & Wildlife agents worked a 16-month sting, much like the one I describe in fiction. They even had the mobile service. I couldn't resist. What a great story! What I added was the part about the owls, though it is truly another real life issue.

The popularity of the Harry Potter books and movies has created a black market for snowy owls across the world. Most are sold in Indonesia and India, but the U.K. and the U.S. are not exempt. This isn't the first time animals have been trafficked due to a rise in interest spurred by Hollywood. The demand for clownfish spiked following the release of *Finding Nemo*—despite the movie's conservation message. Similar trends were seen for green iguanas following the release of *Jurassic Park* and for red-eared sliders from the *Teenage Mutant Ninja Turtles.*

The theory that we love and will protect that which we know isn't a bad one. The problem is, mere exposure is not enough. Even for films that tell an ecological tale, the effects of familiarity actually increase demand in the pet trade. It's consumerism at its worse. Every little kid in America wants his or her own *Nemo*.

Educating people about the harm it does is a step in the right direction.

I hope you enjoyed the story.

Thank YOU for reading. If you're interested in connecting with me online, I like to share travel stories (like my own snowshoeing adventures) and videos (Have you ever seen a napping sloth? This is exciting stuff!), my wildlife photos, and MORE! Please sign up for my newsletter at www. KimberliBindschatel.com. You'll be the FIRST to know about my new releases, too. (I have a special sign-up gift for you.) Join the adventure.

THANK YOU

During the writing of this story, I had help from some wonderful people. Special thanks go to Hannah at Alaska Raptor Center for patiently teaching me about owl behavior and to the Snapp family at Snapp's Taxidermy who kindly gave me a tour and answered all my questions.

To Rachel, as always, for keeping me focused.

I am so thankful for my early readers—April, Linda, and Alexa. And my proof readers went above and beyond—Linda, Benetta, Cathy, Chris, Annie, Lisa, Dawn, Amy, and Jan.

A special thank you to my loving and supportive husband. As always, thanks to my parents for raising me with a deep love of animals.

Thank YOU for reading. If you feel as strongly as I do about the issues presented in this book and you want to help, PLEASE tell a friend about the story. Help me spread the word. You, too, can make a difference! For the animals!

If you'd like to be the FIRST to know about my new releases, please sign up for my newsletter at www.KimberliBindschatel. com. Plus, I share travel stories and videos, my wildlife photos, and MORE! Join the adventure.

About the Author

Kimberli A. Bindschatel is a thrill seeker, travel adventurer, passionate animal lover, wildlife photographer and award-winning author of the Amazon Best-selling Poppy McVie Mystery series.

When she's not busting bad guys with her pen, she's out in the wilderness getting an adrenaline fix. She has rappelled down a waterfall in Costa Rica, rafted the Grand Canyon, faced down an Alaskan grizzly bear at ten feet (camera in hand), snorkeled with stingrays, and white-water kayaked a Norwegian river. She's always ready for an adventure.

She lives in northern Michigan where she loves to hike in the woods with her rescue dog, Josee, share a bottle of wine with good friends, or sail Lake Michigan with her husband on their boat, Priorities. (You gotta have your priorities!)

Kimberli also co-writes the Charity Styles Caribbean Thriller series with Best-selling author, Wayne Stinnett.

She loves sharing her passion for adventure and wildlife with her readers and happily gives away some of her award-winning wildlife photos. Sign up for her newsletter at www.kimberlibindschatel.com and get a free photograph for your desktop.

Join the adventure.

What will Poppy do next?

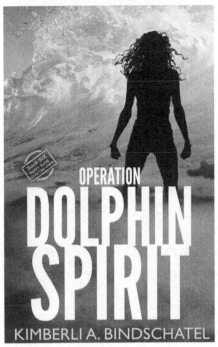

OPERATION
DOLPHIN SPIRIT
KIMBERLI A. BINDSCHATEL

A dark plot in exotic Bimini...
...wild dolphins used for unthinkable ends.
Feisty agent Poppy McVie is willing to risk it all to stop it.

When Poppy is sent with her handsome partner Dalton to evaluate why a pod of dolphins in Bimini is behaving strangely, an easy assignment of sun, beaches, and trade winds quickly turns ugly when nothing is as it seems. When she's told to stand down she suspects the worst, and embarks on a high-stakes operation of her own to get to the bottom of things.

Poppy discovers the truth about the sea creatures and finds herself facing a formidable adversary. Left alone, she has only one chance to stop a clandestine scheme that could change the world order. Can she pull it off with no plan and no backup, or will this mission be her last?